Alice-Miranda in the Outback

Books by Jacqueline Harvey

Alice-Miranda in the Outback

Jacqueline Harvey

PUFFIN BOOKS

PUFFIN BOOKS

UK | USA | Canada | Ireland | Australia
India | New Zealand | South Africa | China

Penguin
Random House
Australia

Penguin Random House Australia is part of the Penguin Random
House group of companies whose addresses can be found at
global.penguinrandomhouse.com.

First published by Puffin Books, an imprint of Penguin Random House
Australia Pty Ltd, in 2020

Cover and internal illustrations by J.Yi
Cover design by Mathematics xy-1.com © Penguin Random House Australia
Pty Ltd
Typeset in 13/18 pt Adobe Garamond by Midland Typesetters, Australia

Printed and bound in Australia by Griffin Press, part of Ovato, an accredited
ISO AS/NZS 14001 Environmental Management Systems printer

A catalogue record for this
book is available from the
National Library of Australia

IISBN 978 1 76 089103 9 (Paperback)

Penguin Random House Australia uses papers that are natural and
recyclable products, made from wood grown in sustainable forests.
The logging and manufacture processes are expected to conform
to the environmental regulations of the country of origin.

penguin.com.au

For Ian and Sandy, and my mother-in-law Joan —
who some years ago, at the age of 84, accompanied
Alice-Miranda and me to central Australia on
our very own outback adventure.

Acknowledgement of Country
I acknowledge the Traditional Owners of
Australia and pay my respects to the Elders,
past, present and future. It is upon their
lands that this story takes place.

Prologue

Barnaby Lewis crouched down on the bank and cupped his hands into the sludgy pool at the bottom of the near-empty dam. It should have been full, or near to it, given it was topped up automatically from one of the bores. He tipped the murky water over his head while beside him, old Kingy took a slurp – though he looked as if he was thinking better of it. The gelding's tail swished and Kingy blinked an eyeful of flies away, only to have them return a second later.

The troughs in the home paddock were drying faster than the washing on the line too. Barnaby had checked the irrigation pipes there yesterday. There had been no obvious holes – no unforeseen puddles to indicate a leak. The bore must have broken down. He stood up and ran his right hand through his thick, dark hair then shoved his Akubra back on his head. The sun was already burning his cheeks and it had only just gone eight. Barnaby couldn't repair the bore alone and manpower was thin on the ground at the moment.

Evie had been away for almost a week now. Barnaby hated the idea of his wife having to deal with so much on her own – selling her parents' home in Sydney, clearing it out and moving her mother into care, but being an only child, the responsibility fell to her. It couldn't be put off any longer, given her father had died suddenly a couple of years ago and her mother was showing early signs of dementia.

With Molly, Ralph and their family away on Sorry Business, Barnaby hadn't been able to leave Hope Springs – not with the mustering about to start as well. Ralph's uncle had passed away three weeks ago and their mob had gone north. Barnaby wasn't sure how long it would be until they got back, but he hoped it was soon. He missed them – Molly especially, and not just because his culinary repertoire was limited to charred meat and three vegetables.

He'd been thinking about her a lot lately – the woman who had mothered him all his life. Born and raised on Hope Springs Station, Molly had never lived anywhere else. After marrying Ralph, she'd had three sons – Clinton, Sam and Buddy – who Barnaby thought of as his big brothers. The boys had grown up doing everything together. Riding, hunting, mustering and camping out bush any chance they could get. Two of them were still here – Sam, with his wife, Rosie, and their kids, River and Storm, and Buddy on his own. Clinton had hit the road years ago, showing up every now and then with stories of where he'd been.

Like his father before him, Barnaby had been sent away to boarding school as a twelve-year-old. He'd spent the first year sobbing into his pillow most nights and longing for the holidays that would take him home to Hope Springs and his beloved Molly and the boys. After university, armed with a degree in agricultural economics, he came home for good and took over the place entirely not long after. Hope Springs had been in Barnaby's family for six generations and he loved it in a way that only someone who was born and bred in the outback could. His own son, Hayden, wasn't interested in the land. The boy dreamt of taking to the skies, but Illaria – his little firebrand daughter, all blonde curls and coffee skin, who preferred to be known only as Larry – said she was never leaving and Barnaby believed her.

Dust swirled in the distance. Barnaby couldn't be sure if it was a vehicle or a willy willy stirring up the red dirt until he saw a glint of silver – a reflection in the sun. There was no one left on the station except him and the kids, so why was there a car in the north paddock? It wasn't some-where even the dopiest of travellers could lose themselves. There *was* an old stock route someone might have been mad enough to follow that came out near the top of Lake Eyre. He'd wait for the call on the two-way – and rescue whoever it was if necessary. Hopefully by road. He'd always been an anxious flyer and preferred not to take the chopper up if he didn't have to.

Barnaby shivered despite the heat. For a second it reminded him of that silly saying about someone walking over your grave. He took up Kingy's reins and stepped into the stirrup when the phone in his top pocket rang. Barnaby pulled it out and squinted at the screen. At least these days they had some coverage if the weather was clear and the satellite was pointing in the right direction. There was a name he hadn't seen in a while.

He pressed the button and answered.

'G'day, Hugh,' he said.

Chapter 1

Alice-Miranda focused on the long, straight stretch of road. In the distance she could see something flying towards them. She wondered for a moment if it was a light aircraft before realising it was an eagle. Another giant bird swooped in from the left across their path, almost touching the bonnet of the four-wheel drive.

'Wow!' Millie exclaimed, having just seen the creatures from the back seat. 'Was that a pterodactyl?'

Alice-Miranda grinned. 'I was thinking the same thing.'

Hugh Kennington-Jones chuckled. 'They say everything is bigger in the outback.'

Millie grabbed her camera from the seat beside her. She was keen to enter the art and photography competition Miss Grimm had announced just before the holidays. There were great prizes as well as the opportunity to be exhibited at the opening of the new Fayle Art Space. Professor Winterbottom, the Fayle School Headmaster, had initiated the idea with Miss Grimm, amid a flurry of excitement and heightened activity in both schools' art rooms. By the time Millie went to take the photograph, though, the birds were too far away.

Behind them, Hugh could see the second Landcruiser in the distance.

'How about we stop and have something to eat?' Hugh asked the girls. 'There should be a roadhouse coming up. Why don't you let your uncle know that's the plan?'

Alice-Miranda picked up the handset from the cradle of the two-way radio and pressed the button on the side.

There was a crackle of static.

'This is KJ One calling Ridley One, do you copy? Over.'

They'd decided on their call signs before setting off from Alice Springs that morning.

'Loud and clear, KJ One,' Lucas replied. 'What can we do for you? Over.'

'We're taking a break at the Kulgera Roadhouse,' Alice-Miranda said, having consulted the paper map she had spread out across her lap. 'Over.'

'Gotcha,' Lucas replied. 'I'm starving and Dad is too. Jacinta's asleep. Can you hear her snoring? Over.'

There was a pause and the sound of Lucas shuffling around in his seat before the girl's breathy grunts came through the airwaves loud and clear.

'Ask him when they picked up the pig,' Millie giggled.

'That's mean, Lucas and Millie. Over,' Alice-Miranda chided, but Millie and Hugh were both laughing.

'You'd better not tell her that I did that. She'll never speak to me again. Over,' Lucas said.

It was another ten kilometres before a clump of iron-roofed buildings loomed into view. A stripped-down sedan sat on a concrete plinth out front, a sign for the Kulgera Hotel perched in the lidless boot. The tyres and doors of the yellow vehicle were missing and a forty-four gallon drum shored up the rear end so it didn't topple from its perch.

'I think that car's seen better days,' Alice-Miranda commented as her father pulled up to one of the petrol pumps that sat beneath a tall awning. Lawrence pulled in to the one behind.

'Sure has,' Millie agreed.

Hugh stepped out of the car and about a thousand flies zoomed in.

'Come on,' Millie said, swatting at the swarm. 'Maybe we should put the windows down. Hopefully they'll leave before we have to get back inside.'

Alice-Miranda jumped down onto the gravel while Lucas and Jacinta hopped out of the car behind them. Jacinta was yawning and stretching her arms, clearly having just woken up.

'How was your nap?' Millie asked Jacinta, who frowned and cast a curious look in Lucas's direction.

'Who said I've been asleep?' Jacinta asked.

'Yawning, stretching, messy hair – bit of a dead giveaway,' Millie replied, giving Lucas a wink. The boy smiled back at her.

'Oh, yeah. Well, I was tired and there is *nothing* to see out here.' The girl rolled her eyes.

'Really? You've missed lots of interesting things,' Alice-Miranda chimed in. 'Like an emu with six chicks running along the side of the road. They were so cute and terribly fast.'

'And a herd of camels and two pterodactyls, which flew right across the bonnet of the car,' Millie said. 'You should have seen them – I wish I'd had the camera out in time.'

Jacinta screwed up her nose. 'Pterodactyls? Really? But I thought they were extinct.'

'Nope,' Millie shook her head and looped her arm through Jacinta's, guiding her towards the roadhouse. She was going to have some fun with this.

Hugh and Lawrence followed the children inside and together they ordered an array of toasted sandwiches, burgers and chips. They were planning to stock up on drinks and snacks too. It was still another four hours before Coober Pedy, their stopover for the night.

'So,' said the woman behind the counter. She wore a sleeveless shirt, showing off arms the size of Christmas hams with a faded tattoo of a rose on her left bicep. Her dark curls were streaked with grey and her face was red – which, upon closer inspection, you could see was the result of broken capillaries that trailed across her skin like a topographical map through the wrinkles. Her name badge said Sharon. 'Whaddaya think of Kulgera, kids?'

'You have some interesting garden ornaments outside,' Alice-Miranda said. Along with the remains of the yellow car there was a huge beer can with four 'X's on it, a sign with the distances from the pub to places all over Australia and a Hills hoist laden with discarded sandshoes and trainers all hanging by their laces like some sort of sporty fruit.

'When I'm not looking after the shop I like to indulge my passion for design,' the woman said, deadpan. Alice-Miranda couldn't tell if she was joking or not. Perhaps the decoration was a particular outback style that Sharon specialised in.

Millie and Jacinta had finished gathering their snacks, along with another tube of sunscreen for Millie to add to the three she'd packed from home – desperate as she was not to get sunburnt on the trip. They brought their haul back to the counter when Jacinta squealed. Alice-Miranda turned to see a large jar containing a dead snake preserved in formaldehyde, and another smaller container that looked to be full of scorpions and various oversized insects. In front of those was a plastic terrarium with the words, 'WARNING DON'T TOUCH – Western Brown Snake' scrawled in permanent marker on the front.

'Phil won't hurt you, love. He's been dead for years,' Sharon said, tapping the lid of the jar. 'But I won't vouch for that other little blighter.' She gestured at the terrarium.

Alice-Miranda leaned in close to see the small brown reptile staring at her, its tongue flicking back and forth. 'Wouldn't he be more comfortable outside in his own environment?' she asked the woman.

'He might be, but I wouldn't,' Sharon said. 'Found him in the guest laundry last week. He can stay right here until Wally – that's my husband, the cook – has time to take him for a ride far, far away. That was Phil's downfall – tried to cosy up to one of the guests in number six as I recall. Woman screamed like a banshee – scared the old fella straight out under a road train. Thought I'd preserve him to show visitors the wildlife that's best avoided.'

Millie gulped.

'Where you kids headed?' Sharon asked, while Wally – tall and nearly bald with heavily tattooed muscly arms – flipped their burgers in the kitchen behind her. He lifted a large stainless steel basket full of chips from the fryer, then slapped them onto a sheet of paper and gave the portion a liberal sprinkling of salt before wrapping it all up and putting the parcel on the counter.

'Coober Pedy, then Hope Springs Station,' Lucas replied.

'Whaddaya doin' out there?' Wally asked sharply, and wiped the sweat from his brow with the back of his hand.

'We're going to help Uncle Barnaby with the mustering,' Alice-Miranda explained. 'Aunt Evie and everyone else is away so Daddy offered that we could give him a hand and it was just fortunate things worked out with our school break.'

'Who's away?' Wally asked.

'Molly and Ralph and their family,' Alice-Miranda said. 'I haven't met them yet, but Daddy's told us a bit about them. He lived on Hope Springs for a while during his gap year – but that was a long time ago.'

'Yeah, right,' Wally mumbled and went back to the grill.

'Have you and Wally lived out here for long?' Alice-Miranda asked Sharon.

'All our lives,' the woman replied. 'Both born and bred in the outback, and never been anywhere else.'

'You must love it then,' the child said.

'Yeah, Wal and I can't get enough of workin' a hundred hours a week for whining travellers who are always complainin', isn't that right, darl?'

The man muttered something. Alice-Miranda couldn't quite make it all out, but it didn't sound like a ringing endorsement of his wife's words.

Millie realised the woman had a gift for sarcasm. 'Where would you rather be?' she asked.

Sharon turned and looked at Wally. 'We're retirin' and headin' for the Greek Islands as soon as our ship comes in. And it's about to set sail – place is sold, so hopefully the next time you're round these parts, we won't be seein' you.'

'I've heard the Greek Islands are lovely, but it's beautiful out here too,' Millie said. 'I don't think

14

photographs do the place justice. The red earth is spectacular and flying over the West MacDonnell Ranges was so colourful – green and red and flowers too, which I hadn't expected.'

'Yeah there's a lot more vegetation than most people think,' Sharon said. 'We had some good rain a few months back. Todd River was flowing in Alice – doesn't happy all that often. Turns the countryside every colour of the rainbow but its dryin' out again now.'

'You ever gonna stop yapping, Shazza?' Wally growled, and threw a tea towel over his shoulder. 'Those kids could starve to death, you know.'

Alice-Miranda looked at the man. He had the air of someone who'd been dealt a rough hand in life.

Wally finished wrapping the last of their order and Sharon rang up the purchases on the till. Lawrence walked to the counter and added several drinks, then pulled out his credit card.

Sharon looked up at him, a flicker of recognition in her eyes. She continued staring then snapped her fingers. 'You're that bloke from the movies. The one in that musical – what was it called again? About Nellie someone or other.'

'*Frontier Woman: The Life and Times of Nellie Williams*,' Jacinta chimed in, her face beaming. 'We were all in –'

'Worst movie I've ever seen,' Sharon interrupted the girl, and rolled her eyes. 'What were you thinking? A musical set in the outback – no one's gonna get excited about that, not to mention it was the Grand Canyon, wasn't it? So not even the proper outback either. And those kids almost did my head in – except the pair that were gun riders. Those girls were the only thing that didn't make me want to poke my own eyes out.'

Millie covered her mouth to stop herself laughing. '*Those girls*' were her and Alice-Miranda, but she wasn't about to say so after Sharon's scathing assessment. The movie had received rave reviews and made a fortune at the box office, but you couldn't please everyone. Hugh was biting his lip and trying not to laugh too.

'Seeing as though you're here,' Sharon continued, 'and I presume you've been in some other films that haven't tanked, how 'bout a picture for the wall.'

Lawrence had remained tight-lipped during Sharon's appraisal. He'd found it was better in these situations to simply nod and maintain a quiet dignity.

The woman bustled out from behind the counter and grabbed the actor, dragging him through an open door and into what looked like a bar area. The children began to follow, but Lawrence suggested they should stay put.

'Things you really don't need to see in here, kids,' Lawrence called out.

'Like what?' Millie asked, craning her neck.

Caps of all colours were hanging from the ceiling, and peppered among them was another unusual decorative touch – an array of bras and undies.

Millie nudged Jacinta and cringed. 'Did you see the size of those bloomers in there? They're bigger than Myrtle Parker's.'

The adults re-emerged, Lawrence shaking Sharon from his arm.

'You might not be the world's best actor, but you are easy on the eye,' the woman said, giving Lawrence a grin.

The group gathered their purchases and made for the door. 'Lovely to meet you all,' Lawrence said through gritted teeth.

'It was Hope Springs you said you were headed, wasn't it?' Sharon called after them.

The family turned and nodded.

'Why?' Hugh asked.

'No, nothing.' The woman shook her head. But Alice-Miranda didn't miss the strange look that passed between Sharon and her husband. Something had been left unsaid.

Chapter 2

It took until the border between the Northern Territory and South Australia to shoo all the flies out of the cars, except then Hugh and Lawrence pulled over so the group could take some photos standing beside the border sign and, quick as a flash, more swarms entered.

Everyone wanted pictures to prove they'd tackled part of the remote wilderness of the vast Australian continent – even if, so far, they'd been driving on a tar-sealed road. That would change once they headed north-east of Coober Pedy.

The trip had come as a surprise to the children, who had just started school holidays. When Hugh had called his old friend Barnaby, only to be told that the man was literally running Hope Springs on his own at the moment – including looking after Hayden and Larry – it had given Hugh an idea. He could afford to take a few weeks off, and there was something about the Australian outback that he couldn't resist.

His brother-in-law, Lawrence, had just wrapped filming on a big superhero movie and joined Charlotte, Lucas and the twins at Highton Hall for a break. When Hugh suggested the trip, Lawrence had jumped at the chance. Charlotte decided that she would stay put with Marcus and Imogen and spend some time with Granny Valentina.

Jacinta had been staying with Alice-Miranda while her mother, Ambrosia, was away covering Fashion Week in Milan with Alice-Miranda's mother, Cecelia, who was doing the buying for the next Highton's Collection. Both women were happy to sit out the dusty holiday. Once the plans were in place, Alice-Miranda had called

Millie's parents. Hamish and Pippa, who had both enjoyed outback experiences of their own in their early twenties, were more than happy for their girl to go along.

'I haven't seen Uncle Barnaby and Aunt Evie for such a long time,' Alice-Miranda said as Hugh pulled out onto the highway. 'I probably wasn't much more than six.'

The last time the families had been together was in Singapore, when they had each been taking a few days break after separate business trips. The Lewises hadn't brought their children, though, so while Alice-Miranda had heard a lot about Hayden and Larry, she'd only ever met them when she was very little and couldn't remember much.

Hugh and Barnaby had known each other since high school, when Hugh had spent a year on exchange at Barnaby's boarding school. The pair were roommates and had hit it off immediately. Hugh had then gone to stay at Hope Springs for eight months during his gap year. These days he made a point of phoning his friend at least once every few months – the outback was a harsh place to raise a family and although Barnaby was an accomplished grazier and stockman, Hugh kept in touch as often as he could. He remembered the isolation well. He'd been a bit remiss with the communication lately though, and was very glad that he'd called when he did.

Back on the highway, Millie was making it her mission to rid the car of its most recent throng of freeloaders. 'Get out of here.' She swatted at another fly that had landed on the top of the drink bottle she was balancing on her thigh while reading from her outback guide book.

'It says that Coober Pedy is the largest opal mining area in the world. It's got such a harsh climate that most people prefer to live in caves bored into the hillsides called dugouts. Temperatures frequently exceed forty degrees Celsius, with little rain. Sounds horrible.'

'We'll be okay,' Alice-Miranda said. 'We're staying at a place called Dinky Di's Dugout – it looks cool.'

'I hope so,' Hugh said. 'I remember how hot it was when I was living on Hope Springs. We've definitely come at the best time of year. Winter is far more preferable to summer, and it will still be warm anyway.'

'Great. I really don't want to get sunburnt and

add any more freckles to my nose,' Millie said, as she coaxed another fly to the top of the window, quickly putting the glass down just a smidge to shoo it out.

The red, flat landscape hadn't really changed much for miles, although there seemed to be an increasing amount of road kill the closer they got to Coober Pedy. Bloated kangaroos and even the odd emu dotted the highway verges and the roadway.

'Look at that eagle.' Millie pointed at a bird standing atop a dead kangaroo in the centre of the road. It was tearing at the animal's flesh and didn't seem remotely concerned about the oncoming car, waiting until the last second before it flapped its giant wings and lifted into the sky.

In the vehicle behind them, Jacinta sat in the centre of the back seat, staring at the road.

'Whoa!' she gasped. 'That must be one of those pterodactyls Millie saw earlier! I thought they were extinct but she was right – they're real.'

Lawrence turned and grinned at his son.

'Should we tell her?' Lucas whispered.

Lawrence arched an eyebrow. 'Let's not spoil things just yet.'

Fortunately Jacinta wasn't paying the least bit of attention to Lucas and his father. She'd turned her head and was staring out the dusty rear window of the car to watch the bird land back on the roo behind them.

'Wait until I tell Mummy.' She shook her head in wonder.

In the car ahead, Alice-Miranda opened the map of South Australia on her knees and ran her finger along the road. 'The dog fence must be coming up soon.'

'I just read about that in my guide book,' Millie said. 'It's amazing to think that it runs all the way from the coast of South Australia through the outback along the New South Wales border and almost to the coast of Queensland. Here,' she flipped back to the page and read. 'It was finished in 1885 and is 5614 kilometres long. Twenty-three people patrol it in 300 kilometre sections.'

'Does it really keep the dingoes out?' Alice-Miranda asked.

Hugh nodded. 'There are stories of stations losing thousands of sheep a year before the fence was finished. It's not perfect, but I imagine it helps considerably. Most of the dingoes stay north of the fence. I know Barnaby still has trouble with wild dogs at Hope Springs, though. I guess when you're dealing with such vast tracts of land it's impossible to know exactly what animals are out here.'

'Or people,' Alice-Miranda said.

Millie leaned forward in her seat. 'What do you mean?'

'Well, when you live on a property that's something like a million acres it would be hard to keep track of everyone who passed through. There are entire countries that are smaller than that. We think Highton Hall is pretty big, but it's tiny compared to things here.'

'True,' Millie said. 'Who else lives out there apart from the Lewises, Hugh?'

'Molly and Ralph help take care of the place with two of their sons and a daughter-in-law. It's only a handful of staff compared to the old days, though. There are photographs of times when they had more than fifty men working the property on horses, but motorbikes and helicopters have replaced much of the manpower now.'

'Will we get to do some mustering?' Alice-Miranda asked.

Her father nodded. 'Sure will. Molly and Ralph and their family are away on Sorry Business and Barnaby's not sure when they'll be back. He can't get that job done on his own – it takes a team to bring the cattle in.'

'What's Sorry Business?' Millie asked.

'It's a time of mourning where Indigenous people attend funerals or participate in other cultural events when someone dies or there is a great sadness. Families and the community get together to make sure that a loved one's spirit is properly put to rest,' Hugh said. 'It's very important.'

'Do you know what Molly and Ralph's Sorry Business is about?' Alice-Miranda asked.

Hugh glanced across at his daughter. 'Ralph's uncle passed away. He was a highly regarded Elder in the community.'

For a few moments the car fell silent.

Alice-Miranda finally spoke. 'I think Sorry Business is a good name for times like that.'

'Yeah, me too,' Millie agreed. She was staring out of the window and spotted a small sign just in front of them. 'Hey, that's the dog fence.'

Hugh braked hard and pulled off the road. Fortunately Lawrence had plenty of time to come to a stop alongside.

'It's a wonder people don't shoot straight past,' Alice-Miranda said.

Given the skid marks on the road, apparently lots of drivers did.

The sign was not much more than an old white piece of sheet metal with a handwritten explanation. It stood on two skinny metal posts and there were two discarded tyres in front.

'How come it says that it's 9600 kilometres long?' Millie asked. 'The guide book says it's only 5614.'

Alice-Miranda shrugged. 'We'll have to do some more research. Either way, that's still a very long fence,' the girl said.

There was a crackle of static through the radio.

'Ridley One to KJ One – anyone want to get out?' Lawrence asked. 'I'm not keen about filling the car with flies. Over.'

'I agree,' Millie said. 'I've only just got rid of the last lot.' She picked up her camera from the back seat and passed it to Alice-Miranda.

Hugh took the handset from the cradle. 'KJ One to Ridley One, photo from inside the vehicle on this occasion. Wimps in here don't want to deal with flies again either. Over.'

Lucas and Jacinta gave a thumbs up while Alice-Miranda snapped several shots.

Lawrence and Hugh nodded at one another and they set off again. There was thirty kilometres to go until Coober Pedy and, although the drive hadn't been as arduous as Hugh had predicted, they had been on the road for almost eight hours.

It wasn't long before Hugh turned left off the highway, just past an antiquated truck sitting atop a metal frame with a sign that told them they'd reached their destination. Hugh explained to the girls that the truck was called a blower, even though its job was more like a giant vacuum unit. There was an array of other interesting signs too – warning visitors about the dangers of mine areas and the penalties for entering claims uninvited.

Unlike Kulgera, which only had the roadhouse with the pub and some accommodation, a police station and other disused outbuildings, Coober Pedy was a proper town. There were plenty of houses above ground, with huge square air-conditioning units balanced on their tin roofs. Mismatched corrugated iron fences divided the properties. There was no grass except for at the school, next to the town swimming pool, and the trees were mostly small and scrubby looking.

'I thought people lived underground out here,' Millie said, wondering where those dwellings were. 'It all looks pretty normal to me.'

'You'd think that, wouldn't you,' Hugh said. 'But believe me, they're here. You just have to know what to look for.'

'I think that's one!' Alice-Miranda exclaimed, pointing to an enclosed porch, with a front door and small window beside it, that looked as if someone had tacked it onto the front of a cliff face.

They passed another structure that appeared to be a tiny shed, but it was so narrow it had to lead to a dugout behind.

'What a strange place,' Millie said. 'And where are the mines?'

'All over,' Hugh replied. 'You never walk backwards in Coober Pedy, or you might find yourself down a disused shaft. See those conical mounds of earth,' he pointed towards the edge of town, where the landscape was dotted with them. 'They're called mullock heaps – that's the dirt

29

and rock that's been pulled out of the ground. If that's how much earth is on the surface, you can only imagine how many holes there are.'

Millie's eyebrows shot up as she surveyed the odd landscape.

Hugh drove to the main street and pulled into a parking space outside a row of shops, several of them dedicated to opals. Across the road was a supermarket, the post office and a hardware store.

'Can we get something to eat?' Alice-Miranda asked. The hamburger at Kulgera seemed a long time ago.

'Perhaps we'll see if the bakery has anything for afternoon tea. We can have an early dinner too – I hear The Outback Bar and Grill is the place to go,' Hugh said. 'But before that, I was thinking we might head up the hill and see if we can find old Sprocket.'

'Who's that?' Millie asked.

'You'll see,' Hugh said with a grin.

Chapter 3

A short while later, the family set off to the outskirts of town full of vanilla slices and lamingtons, as well as milkshakes for the children and coffee for Hugh and Lawrence. On the way to Sprocket's, they saw mullock heaps everywhere, and strange cylinders with little hats that Hugh explained were ventilation shafts for the mines and dugouts.

'So how do you know this person, Hugh?' Millie asked.

The man made a left turn and drove slowly along the roadway, obviously looking for something.

'Sprocket saved my life,' Hugh said.

Alice-Miranda's eyebrows jumped up. She couldn't remember ever having heard this story before.

'How?' the child asked. 'You didn't fall down a mine shaft did you?'

'Something like that. But best leave Sprocket to tell the story. He's much better at it than I am,' Hugh said, a glint in his eye. 'Ah, here we are.' He pointed at a sign that said 'Sprocket's Hideaway' and made a right turn into a gravel driveway that wound up onto a small plateau. Hugh backed the car beside an old truck and a tractor. Lawrence pulled in next to them.

Opposite the cars, built into the side of the rock was a tiny, crooked tin shed with a flat roof and front door. Alice-Miranda thought there must be a dugout on the other side. It was so small, she couldn't imagine more than a couple of people could fit within its walls.

'Shouldn't you have called first?' Alice-Miranda asked. 'Mummy wouldn't approve of us arriving unannounced. What if Mr Sprocket's busy?'

Hugh opened his mouth to reply when suddenly the plateau was shaken by a loud explosion. A plume of rocks and dust flew into the sky, debris crashing onto the top of the shed while more rained down in front of the cars. It was lucky only some small pieces of grit hit the bonnets.

Seconds later, a skinny, bearded figure dressed in a blue singlet and shorts, and with a bright orange terry towelling hat, came running over the top of a mullock heap. He had thongs on his feet and his weedy limbs were the colour of snow, as if they'd rarely seen the sun.

'You little ripper!' he shouted punching the air. 'What a bewdy!'

Apparently he hadn't spotted the two Landcruisers or the bemused occupants watching his antics from inside. He hurried over to inspect a fist-sized lump of rock that had ricocheted off the top of the shed. 'Maybe one less stick next time – don't want to put a hole in the roof.'

Hugh opened the car door and stepped out.

'Sprocket!' he called.

The man stuck his fingers in his ears and gave them a jiggle. Perhaps the explosion had affected his hearing.

Hugh turned back to the girls and smiled then walked closer to the man who was now parading around like an emu, picking up the rocks that had plummeted and closely inspecting each one before throwing them away again.

'Do you think he's looking for opals?' Millie asked. 'Is it that easy to find them?'

Alice-Miranda shrugged. 'He's certainly looking for something.'

'Hello Sprocket,' Hugh called again. This time the man spun around and immediately fell backwards to the ground, his legs lifting to the sky as if he'd fainted.

Alice-Miranda leapt out of the car and ran towards her father.

'Daddy, is he all right? Should we call an ambulance?' She knelt beside the man.

Hugh winked and shook his head. Curiously, Sprocket opened one eye for about three seconds before closing it and opening the other. Alice-Miranda was stunned to see they were the most dazzling shade of blue. Then he squeezed both eyes shut, opened them and sat bolt upright.

'Well, blow me down, if it isn't my old mate Hugh with Two.' The fellow grinned, revealing an impossibly white set of teeth. Alice-Miranda hadn't been expecting that. She shielded her eyes from the glare.

'Sorry,' the man apologised. 'Had a good year a couple back and decided to treat myself to some new choppers – whiter than a whale's tooth, if you ask me.'

Alice-Miranda giggled. 'Hello sir, my name is Alice-Miranda Highton-Smith-Kennington-Jones and I'm very pleased to meet you.' She offered her hand. He took it and stood up.

'Sprocket McGinty at your service, young lady,' the miner replied. Then he turned to Hugh and gave the man a hearty hug. 'Blimey, I thought your name was bad enough, Hugh with Two, and you've gone and given the poor kid four and more.'

'Hugh with Two – does that refer to Daddy's surname?' Alice-Miranda frowned.

'He's never called me anything else,' Hugh said. 'I guess it has a certain ring to it.'

Sprocket brushed the red dirt from his white shorts and took his thongs off, clapping them together and creating a cloud of dust before dropping them and jamming them back on his dirty feet. 'You should have called, mate. I'd have baked a cake. But reception's dodgy and the oven's been busted for seven years, so that's a lie, but I hope you've been to the bakery – one of Nancy's vanilla slices wouldn't go astray right about now.'

Alice-Miranda giggled again. She'd wondered why her father had ordered another round of takeaway cakes. She ran to get the box from the front seat and beckoned for Millie and the others to join her. They hopped out of the cars and trotted over.

'Were you blasting a new mine shaft, Mr McGinty?' Alice-Miranda asked as she passed her father the box of treats.

'A new mine?' Sprocket looked at the girl blankly.

'The explosion?' the child said.

'No, I'm putting in a sunroom,' he said with a firm nod.

Alice-Miranda didn't know whether to believe him or not. She mulled it over while Hugh introduced the others. 'Well, I can see you're all just as right and proper as my old mate Hugh with Two,' Sprocket said. 'And me with no manners standing here in the sun. Who'd like a cuppa? Might even have some fizzy drink for the kids.

Fridge is still working. And I'm pretty sure that I washed the cups last time I had visitors, but we might check that. It was some time ago.'

The group followed the man to the tiny tin shed, where he opened the door. 'Shoes off,' he said.

Millie nudged Alice-Miranda and the pair began to undo their laces.

'Nah, just kidding. What do you think this is? A palace or something?' Sprocket grinned, and you'd have sworn he'd just turned a light on.

The children could hardly believe their eyes as they followed the man inside. The tiny shed gave way to a large lounge room complete with a television set and a china cupboard. There was a floral settee still covered in plastic and a yellow shag pile rug on the floor. On the wall hung an assortment of mismatched paintings – clearly done by someone with very little skill.

Sprocket noticed the children staring. 'You like my horses?' He pointed at a canvas. 'Took me an age to finish that one. Still not sure if I've got the tail right.'

Millie had to shove her fist in her mouth to stop herself from laughing. The tail was the least of the man's worries, given the horse's head was shaped like a watermelon, but she had to love his enthusiasm.

The dugout wasn't huge, but it wasn't tiny either. It was also cooler inside than out – the lounge room was a very pleasant twenty-three degrees – it said so on the large digital thermometer on the wall.

'This is unexpected,' Lucas said, glancing around.

Sprocket led the group through to the kitchen, which looked much like you'd find in any regular home – although the cupboards were painted a garish orange and the oven had a piece of blue and white police tape crisscrossing the front of it. Jacinta's eyes widened in alarm, wondering why there was a crime scene in the man's kitchen.

'Did something happen here?' she asked quietly.

Sprocket tilted his head like a curious puppy as Jacinta pointed.

'Oh no, that's just to remind me about the broken gas pipe. Don't want to blow myself up, so I asked the Sarge if he could spare some tape. He gave me a whole roll. Excellent for keeping stickybeaks off the claim too,' Sprocket explained. 'It's lucky I gave up smoking years ago – actually I don't think I ever did smoke. It's a filthy habit.'

He filled the kettle with water and set about retrieving cups and saucers from an overhead cupboard.

'We'll give you a hand, Mr Sprocket,' Alice-Miranda said. The crockery looked clean enough, but after the man's earlier comment she thought it was better to give everything a rinse just in case. Millie did the drying.

Hugh had set the box of cakes on the dining room table and he and Lawrence were now hunting for plates.

Sprocket directed Lucas and Jacinta to a side room where he said they'd find another fridge. Sure enough, there were cans of lemonade and cola lining the shelves, so the pair helped themselves to a selection and brought it back to the table.

'Fizzy drink doesn't go off, does it?' Sprocket asked. The children looked at one another and shrugged. The man directed everyone to sit down. Tea and cakes were passed around and, though the children and Lawrence and Hugh had just had afternoon tea, none of them hesitated.

'Mr McGinty,' Alice-Miranda said.

The fellow looked around dramatically. 'Is the ghost of my old dead dad here again?'

Alice-Miranda shook her head. 'No, I was talking to you.'

'No one calls me Mr McGinty unless they're a magistrate,' the man replied.

'Mr Sprocket, Daddy said that you saved his life once.' Alice-Miranda was determined to hear the story her father had begun to share.

'Did he now? Well, it all started one day when this young fella arrived in town en route to Hope Springs. Trouble was, it had been raining for a month and the road was flooded, so he had to stop in Coober Pedy till things dried out. Hugh with Two was down the pub asking about some work and a place to stay. I was there, enjoying a cleansing ale, and I didn't think he looked too bad. Bit of a rough head, but he was young and strongish, so I offered him a bed and brought him up here. Mind you, his bed was on the floor because I hadn't finished the guest room yet, but he didn't seem to care,' Sprocket said. 'He had the fanciest swag I've ever seen – remember it came with snake repellent and all – whoever sold him that saw him coming.'

'So Daddy lived here and worked for you,' Alice-Miranda said.

'I wouldn't go so far as calling it work, but he did a bit and kept out of trouble for a minute or so,' Sprocket explained. 'It was all going well until he decided to use the amenities in the middle of the night.'

'What happened?' Jacinta said.

'Patience,' the man replied. 'Hugh with Two got up for the loo – heck I'm a poet and I didn't even know it,' the man chuckled.

The children giggled, but Lawrence began to wonder if the fellow didn't have a few sheep loose in the top paddock.

'Anyway, the house wasn't nearly as luxurious as it is now, and we still had an external facility. Except that Hugh with Two got confused about which of the outbuildings was the toilet and which was the entrance to one of my old mine shafts. Fell straight in, didn't he. Lucky I always take an evening constitutional to check the claim. That's how I heard him, or who knows how long he'd have been down there – probably still be there now come to think of it. Been a couple of those over the years. Anyway, I'd been using that shaft to store some of my cactus plants until I got the garden going.'

The children looked at Hugh, who winced. He held up his hands to indicate the length of the spines.

'Ow!' They all shuddered.

'I spent the rest of the night removing prickles from your father's bare bottom.'

'I didn't see any cacti out in your yard,' Alice-Miranda said. She couldn't remember seeing any garden at all.

'Once I realised what a danger those beasties were, I got rid of them. Couldn't risk having anyone else with a bum full of prickles,' Sprocket said earnestly.

'So there you have it, kids. Rescued by a mad miner from his killer cacti,' Hugh said. 'And it's something of a miracle, but we've stayed friends ever since – although I think this is only the second time I've seen him since then. It's fortunate country folk don't forget things.'

'He's a good bloke, Hugh with Two. Doesn't really think I'm crazy – not like everyone else around here,' Sprocket said, then immediately changed tack. 'Would you like to have a look at the new seam?'

'Down a mine shaft?' Lucas said.

'Actually, I found it by accident during the renovations. Richest bit of ground I've ever dug up, and to think it only happened because I wanted more room in the dugout,' Sprocket said. 'Come on.'

'So that's what you were working on when we arrived?' Alice-Miranda asked.

'No, was breaking up a slab of stone out the back. Thought I might put in a guest suite. Tourists pay a lot of money to stay in this town so I decided to cash in on the action.'

They followed Sprocket through the kitchen and down a narrow tunnel to another space almost the same size as the lounge room. There was a string of naked globes glowing against the wall, but the old man turned them off and picked up a torch. He shone it around, illuminating a spidery vein of coloured lines.

'Whoa, it's like an Aladdin's Cave,' Millie gasped.

'If it's not rude to ask, do you know how much you could be looking at here?' Lawrence asked.

'Sadly, a lot less than you were paid for that awful musical you were in – yes, you think you can come to the outback and be anonymous, Lawrence Ridley, but I know exactly who you are.

Hollywood royalty.' Sprocket winked at the man. 'Don't worry, I was probably the only person in the world who didn't enjoy it.'

'That's not true,' Jacinta shook her head. 'The lady at the Kulgera Roadhouse said much worse things.'

Alice-Miranda nudged her friend. Jacinta bit her lip, realising her lack of tact. 'Sorry – I didn't mean to be rude.'

Lawrence grinned. 'It's all right, Jacinta. I'd rather know that, even in the middle of nowhere, people have paid good money to see the movie, never mind if they didn't enjoy it.'

Sprocket looked at him in the dim light. 'Paid. You're kidding, right? I've got a satellite dish on my roof that could eavesdrop on the Australian Parliament if I wanted to – which, by the way, I don't, at least not since that incident at Woomera, which we won't talk about now.

'Anyway, in answer to your question, this could make me rich beyond my wildest dreams. But don't you go spreading that around. You never know who's listening and I don't want to end up like Taipan Dan.'

'What happened to him?' Millie asked.

'Gone,' Sprocket said. 'Last time I spoke to the silly old codger he said he was onto something big – the find of his life. I don't really understand him though – he never has a brass razoo, and yet over the years he's probably dug up millions in opals. No idea what he does with his money unless he's got a fortune squirrelled away for a rainy day. But it hardly ever rains out here now does it? I've been waiting three months for him to come back.'

'Do you think he's met with foul play?' Alice-Miranda asked.

Sprocket shrugged.

'Thought I saw his ute in town the other week so I went over to borrow some dynamite, but his place was locked up tighter than a tin can. Still, I managed to get in – did a short stint as a locksmith in my younger years. Anyway, the house was the same as always – washing up in the sink, fridge full of rotten food – except he wasn't there. Only been a coupla times in the past thirty years he's left town and he's always asked me to keep an eye on things. This time – nothing. I checked the claim – he hasn't fallen down a shaft as far as I could see. Nor was he dead on a mound of dirt the way my old mate Harry left the world.'

'What about his car?' Lucas asked, his eyes wide.

'Gone too. And Junie.'

'Is that his wife?' Millie asked.

'No, she's his cat – there's been no wives that I know of,' Sprocket said. 'Oh, and there was one other thing . . .'

Chapter 4

Alice-Miranda stared at the ceiling. Every now and again, depending on which way she turned her head, she could see a sparkle. Sprocket had told the children that it was potch – opal with no colour, and of no value either. Still, it was pretty to look at.

She couldn't help thinking about what might have happened to Taipan Dan – where he'd gone and why he'd disappeared without telling anyone. That seemed a dangerous thing to do in the outback, given the vast distances and isolation. Alice-Miranda had expected it to be big, but now she was actually here she was beginning to realise the enormity of the landscape.

Millie and Jacinta were sound asleep. Alice-Miranda could hear Millie's breathy grunts and Jacinta's not-so-sweet snores.

They'd arrived at their accommodation and been greeted by Di, a smiling blonde lady who was the perfect hostess and lived in her own dugout next door. The woman had kindly stocked the fridge and pantry with bacon, eggs, bread and milk for breakfast, and recommended the Outback Bar and Grill for dinner, which had proven every bit as delicious as they'd hoped.

Alice-Miranda looked at the clock on the bedside table. It had just gone four and, no matter how many sheep she counted in her head, sleep wouldn't come. She pushed back the covers and padded noiselessly to the hallway. Lucas was lying on the pull-out couch in the lounge room.

She nudged past her cousin. It was strange being in a house that was almost entirely underground, although the air still felt fresh inside.

'Can't sleep either?' Lucas whispered.

Alice-Miranda turned around. 'Sorry, I didn't mean to wake you.'

Lucas sat up. 'You didn't. I've been awake for ages.'

'Me too,' the girl said. 'Would you like some water?'

Lucas nodded and hopped up to join her in the kitchen.

'I've been thinking about that guy, Taipan Dan,' Lucas said.

'Yes,' Alice-Miranda said. 'What's your theory?'

'Maybe he's sick and had to go to the city to see some doctors, or maybe it was a family matter,' the boy said.

Alice-Miranda frowned. 'Mr Sprocket sounded worried, and he did say there was something else – and then he never told us what it was.'

The man had been in the middle of his story when he got distracted by a sparkle in the seam. He'd taken his pick and started chipping away, and from that point on it was as if he was mesmerised. After ten minutes or so, Hugh realised it was opal fever, and they weren't going to get another thing out of him. The group had bade Sprocket farewell and made a detour via the kitchen to wash up, leaving the man to his work.

They'd all been disappointed not to hear the rest of the story, but Hugh said it was something he'd got used to in the short time he'd lived there. Sprocket would start a tale and, if he was lucky, Hugh might hear the rest of it a day or so later. Hugh said that he'd never met Taipan Dan – Sprocket had kept to himself during Hugh's previous stay.

'What do you think it could have been?' Lucas asked. 'The thing Sprocket left out.'

'Who knows?' Alice-Miranda said. 'Do you want to look at the stars?'

'Sure,' Lucas said. The waitress at the restaurant had said they were her favourite thing about the outback. But by the time they'd arrived home from dinner, everyone was so tired that they'd forgotten to take a proper look.

Alice-Miranda opened the front door as quietly as she could, and she and Lucas walked out onto the porch. The first thing they both noticed was the chill. While inside was a pleasant twenty-three degrees, the temperature out here couldn't have been more than about six or seven.

The other thing they noticed was the darkness. The dugout had been softly illuminated by a small row of lights under the kitchen cabinets that threw off enough of a glow for the occupants to be able to get around without bumping into things, but now the children found themselves wrapped in a cloak of black. It was almost impossible to see anything at ground level, and yet when they raised their eyes towards the heavens it was as if the most beautiful jewel box in the world had been sprinkled across the sky.

'Wow!' Lucas gasped.

'It's incredible,' Alice-Miranda said.

Two Cape Cod lawn chairs situated just beyond the covered veranda offered a perfect vantage point. Lucas ducked back inside, pulling the quilt from his bed to keep them both warm.

The children sat side by side and tilted their heads skywards. For the next half hour or so they picked out constellations and planets until they fell sound asleep.

They were woken by the warmth of the sun's rays on their cheeks and Millie's voice calling their names.

'We're out here,' Alice-Miranda shouted, and rubbed her eyes.

Millie scrambled through the front door and was surprised to see the pair under the doona in their pyjamas. 'Lucky you're cousins. If Jacinta found you cosied up with anyone else like that, Lucas, the Coober Pedy police would probably be investigating a murder.'

'Don't be ridiculous. Jacinta's not the jealous type,' Lucas said.

Millie and Alice-Miranda looked at one another and raised their eyebrows.

The smell of bacon wafted through the screen door. 'Breakfast's ready,' Lawrence called from inside.

Something on the dusty ground beyond the lawn chairs caught Millie's attention as she turned to the door. 'Don't suppose you noticed the owner of those tracks?'

Alice-Miranda and Lucas hopped up. Millie was pointing at a long trail through the red dirt.

'Looks like it came from right under your chair, Alice-Miranda,' Lucas said. 'Glad it was dark and we didn't see anything.'

Di, the owner of the dugout, gave the children a wave from her front veranda next door.

'Morning, kids,' she called. She walked out

to see what they were looking at. 'Oh, that's a big 'un.'

'Any idea what sort of snake it might have been?' Lucas asked.

Di bent down and looked at the tracks. 'Brown I'd say. Too fat for an inland taipan. Both deadly though, so if you see one get out of its way.'

At the mention of the word taipan, Alice-Miranda thought about Sprocket's story from yesterday. 'Di, do you know a man called Taipan Dan?'

The woman nodded. 'Everyone around here knows of Taipan Dan, though you're not likely to meet him. I haven't set eyes on the man for years. Heard he doesn't leave his place at all these days. Has the groceries delivered to the front gate every couple of months.'

'Why is he called that?' Millie asked.

'The story goes that he lived to tell the tale after being bitten by an inland taipan – the deadliest snake in the world. He'd be one of very few people to have that honour,' the woman said. 'But whether it's true or not is hard to say. The outback is full of tall stories.'

'He sounds like a character,' Alice-Miranda said.

'One of many,' Di said. 'And all with their secrets.'

'We heard that he's missing,' Alice-Miranda said.

'Probably just sniffed out another claim. I wouldn't worry – they all come back sometime, except when they don't,' Di said. 'Anyway, go and enjoy your breakfast, and make sure to keep the screen door closed. Never had a snake inside the dugout, and I'd prefer it stays that way.'

Lucas bundled up the quilt and the three children hurried inside, where Hugh and Lawrence were busy piling lashings of bacon and eggs, toast and tomato onto plates.

The family were packed and ready to leave Di's by half past ten. Hugh and Lawrence decided they'd take the children to some of the underground shops and do a spot of shopping for Cee and Charlotte while they were there. Lucas was keen to get a surprise for Jacinta as well, and he'd asked Alice-Miranda and Millie to distract her while he made his selection. Her birthday was coming up next month and she'd mentioned more than a few times how much she loved opals. They visited the Catacomb Church and the Old Timer's Mine & Museum too before it was nearing time to head off.

Next they made a stop at the grocery shop to pick up a couple of boxes of supplies Barnaby had ordered by phone the day before, and then the last stop was the hardware store. There they collected spare parts for the bores, some feed, tools and various other bits and pieces.

While Hugh and Lawrence headed back into the store to collect the last of their order and Jacinta and Lucas made their way to the bakery to purchase some supplies for the long drive, Millie and Alice-Miranda rearranged the back of the car to make sure everything could fit snugly. Alice-Miranda had just moved the suitcases to make room for the groceries when she spotted a familiar face coming out of the hardware store. A burly man was walking towards them, balancing a box under his arm and clutching a couple of shiny shovels in one hand. A lit cigarette dangled from the other.

'Hello.' She looked up and gave a wave. 'It's Wally, isn't it?' she said.

'Who's askin'?' the man replied gruffly.

Millie looked over and recognised the fellow too. His expression was just as sour as when they'd met him the day before.

'You cooked our lunch yesterday at the roadhouse,' Alice-Miranda replied, thinking it was probably a good thing he and his wife Sharon had sold the business. They didn't seem especially suited to the hospitality trade.

'Must have been all right because you're still alive,' Wally sniped.

'Oh, it was delicious, thank you,' Alice-Miranda said, and she meant it.

'You have to drive a long way to get to the hardware store,' Millie said. 'You wouldn't want to forget anything.'

'A long drive's par for the course when you live out here,' he grouched. 'And I've got everything I need, don't you worry about that. Things are finally coming right for old Wally and Shaz – just one last piece of the puzzle and we're off.'

The girls nodded, not quite sure of what he meant. Although Alice-Miranda remembered that yesterday Sharon had said something about their ship coming in and moving to Greece.

Millie looked across the road and realised there was another great photo opportunity – of rusty roofs and red dirt and plateaus with mullock heaps beyond the shops. She quickly pulled out her camera and aimed the lens at the scene before turning back and absently snapping a picture of Wally as he was walking away – the quintessential outback bloke. Today, he was dressed in a black T-shirt with an open flannelette shirt over the top, a pair of shorts and worn workboots that looked as if they were feasting on his socks. He had a battered Akubra on his head.

She showed Alice-Miranda. 'That's a good one. A true Aussie bushman.'

'Fantastic,' the girl replied, then noticed something on the ground. Wally must have dropped it out of the box he'd been carrying. She bent down to pick it up and realised that it was a compass.

'Did you see where he went?' Alice-Miranda turned back to Millie, who shook her head.

The child ran to the corner and scanned the vehicles angle-parked against the kerb, but Wally was nowhere to be seen. The couple of cars that had just left were now specks in a cloud of red dust.

She spun around.

'Oh well,' Millie said. 'You tried. Bit weird that he was buying shovels and a compass if he's about to leave for Greece, don't you think?'

Alice-Miranda frowned. 'True,' she said, and sat the object on the wall right near where Wally had dropped it. 'Maybe he'll come back – although perhaps I should take it into the shop. I imagine he's more likely to look for it there.'

Millie agreed and the girl raced away returning with her father and Lawrence who had the last of Barnaby's hardware purchases. Jacinta and Lucas appeared too, holding up several large bags full of bakery delights.

'Who was that guy you were talking to?' Lucas asked. He had seen the girls with the man while he and Jacinta were walking back on the other side of the road.

'Wally from the Kulgera Roadhouse,' Millie said. 'He was thrilled to see us.'

Jacinta sneered. 'He wasn't yesterday,' she said, then realised that Millie was being sarcastic. 'Oh, I get it. At least everyone else we've met out here is lovely.'

Alice-Miranda nodded as the family and friends piled back into their cars and set off towards Hope

Springs Station. She was thinking about what Wally had said about having everything he needed. She hoped they did too – it was a long way to turn around and go back to town again.

Chapter 5

Barnaby Lewis hung up the telephone and glanced at the open accounts ledger on the desk. Evie had to be the most stoic woman he'd ever met. True to form, she had been full of questions about the kids, and how he was coping and whether there had been any news from Molly and Ralph. When he asked after her she told him things were going well – although he'd heard a tremble in his wife's voice when she related a moment in which her mother had been terribly upset because she'd forgotten she was moving and was angry at Evie for making her. Barnaby wished he could be there to support her, but the station wouldn't run itself.

Yesterday he and the kids had ridden out to check the troughs again only to find them nigh on empty. The dam was too. The bore was definitely not pumping water where it should – he needed to get it fixed as soon as possible. Thankfully Hugh and his gang of helpers were due this evening. They could head out first thing tomorrow and, with a bit of luck, get the work done within a day.

'How's Mum?' Hayden asked from the study doorway where he was leaning against the frame.

Barnaby looked up. 'Yeah, mate, she's fine – sends her love. Your grandmother's not so good, but Mum still hopes to be home by the end of the month.'

Hayden nodded. The boy pushed his brown fringe out of his eyes. He needed a haircut, but that wasn't going to happen until Molly or his mum got back. He missed them both terribly with a dull ache that swelled in his chest.

'You okay, mate?' Barnaby looked at the boy's sun-kissed face, which was smattered with freckles. It was hard to believe Hayden would be off to boarding school next year, though Barnaby had a feeling his son would enjoy the experience far more than he did. Larry, on the other hand, said that she was never leaving Hope Springs – she'd threatened to chain herself to the washing line when her turn came. She was such an outback kid, like Barnaby had been. Never out of jeans and riding boots, her sandy hair always hanging in two plaits over her shoulders.

'Yeah, I'm fine. Just a bit worried about Mum and Granny, and I miss Molly,' Hayden said.

'Well, that makes two of us,' Barnaby said as he stood up from the desk and walked over to his son. He wrapped his arms around the lad.

'They'll be fine, mate,' Barnaby could feel himself welling up. He had Molly to thank for the fact that he hugged his kids. He couldn't remember his father ever showing him any affection. Not even when his mother left them the day after Barnaby's fifth birthday. It was Molly who had hugged him and made everything okay. He'd watched her and Ralph hug their own boys often. As a young man, Barnaby had vowed that if later on he was blessed with children, he'd do the same.

'What's the matter?' Larry asked urgently as she walked in on the scene. 'Is something wrong with Mum?'

Barnaby released Hayden and looked at his daughter. 'No, she's good. Just tired, and your grandmother isn't making things easy. Sadly, dementia isn't kind to anyone.'

Larry nodded. 'So you were just having a moment. I suppose hugs have been a bit thin on the ground lately with Molly and Mum away.'

Barnaby frowned. 'Hang on a tick. Haven't I tucked you and your brother in every night?'

'Yeah, but Molly's hugs are the best,' Larry said, a glint in her eye.

Barnaby lurched towards the child, picking her up in his arms and twirling her around and around. The girl kissed his cheek. 'I love you, Dad.'

'I love you too, Larry.' He glanced over at Hayden, whose eyes were glistening. 'Come here, mate.'

He hugged the boy with his free arm and the three of them stayed that way for a minute or so before Barnaby wiped his eyes and put Larry down.

'What time is Uncle Hugh coming?' the girl asked.

'I don't imagine they'll be here until mid-afternoon at the earliest,' Barnaby replied, walking over to stand beside his daughter.

Through the French doors that led to the veranda, he noticed a swirl of dust in the distance.

Hayden joined them. 'Maybe it's Molly and Ralph.'

'Well, that would certainly make my day,' Barnaby said.

'Ours too. If we have to eat another burnt sausage for dinner, I think I'll go on a hunger strike.' Larry grinned.

'How about some lunch then? And I promise nothing charred,' Barnaby said.

'Thank goodness for that,' Hayden said.

Barnaby glanced outside again, but the dust had settled. His heart sank a little. Must have been a willy willy.

Chapter 6

'Wow! Look at that!' Alice-Miranda pointed at the flat-topped land formations rising dramatically from the desert floor.

'They're called breakaways,' Millie read from her guide book. 'Once covered by an inland sea, they're now home to an array of native fauna and flora.'

'They're beautiful,' Alice-Miranda said, gazing at the rocky landscape. 'I bet they're even more spectacular at sunrise and sunset.'

'That's exactly what it says here.' Millie ran her finger down the page.

'I'm afraid we don't have time to explore today,' Hugh said. 'Maybe on the way back. We need to get these spare parts out to Hope Springs. I hadn't realised that Barnaby was in such desperate straits with the bore until he sent the message last night.'

They settled in for the long drive. Endless miles of dusty red plains passed by the window, with plenty of animals too. There were emus that ran along the roadside in mobs of six or seven, big red kangaroos foraging for food among the native shrubs and eagles flying across their path, each sighting eliciting excitable radio contact about pterodactyls from Jacinta.

The poor girl would have to wake up sooner or later, but Millie hoped not. This was more fun than seeing a Scottish reporter duped into being kitted out in full body armour and a pair of industrial goggles to handle the (completely fictional) dangerous subspecies of koala called a drop bear. The woman had been completely sucked in by the cheeky fellows who set her up. Then again, Australia was home to some of the strangest animals on earth and had more than its fair share of deadly creatures, so believing in drop bears was actually kind of understandable.

'Let's play I Spy,' Alice-Miranda suggested.

Hugh glanced at his daughter. 'Mmm, okay. But there's not a lot out there.'

'It's an inside-the-car version,' Millie said. 'At least after the first guesses of red dirt and kangaroos and emus and eagles.'

'There's got to be more than that out there,' Alice-Miranda said.

They'd been driving for two hours and hadn't passed a single vehicle after the first twenty minutes. It felt as if they were the only people on the planet – except that this landscape looked more like Mars.

'I spy with my little eye, something beginning with "C",' Alice-Miranda said.

Millie looked outside. She was racking her brain, but nothing came to mind. Hugh looked in the rear-vision mirror and spotted the box of groceries they'd picked up for Barnaby.

'Can, as in tin can, over the back,' Hugh said.

'No, that's not it.' Alice-Miranda shook her head.

Millie was deep in thought when suddenly she exclaimed, 'Cat!'

Alice-Miranda turned and looked at her friend. 'There's no cats out here.'

'Ah, yes there is,' Millie pointed, jiggling about in her seat. 'Hugh, look out!'

A fat ginger cat had just run from a scrubby bush and sat down in the middle of the dirt road. It raised its right paw into the air as if to say 'stop'.

Hugh slammed on the brakes, Lawrence skidding to a halt behind them. Alice-Miranda and Millie both leapt out of the car.

'Girls, be careful,' Hugh shouted as everyone else got out. 'It's likely to be feral.'

Alice-Miranda slowly approached the puss, who meowed loudly.

'Hello, what are you doing here?' She leaned down low and the cat padded towards her. It rubbed its head all over her bare legs and began to purr.

'Not feral, Hugh,' Millie said. 'Looks like someone's pet.'

Alice-Miranda stood up and patted her thighs. The creature jumped into her arms and smooched her face and neck.

The others couldn't believe their eyes.

'Good grief – where did that come from?' Lawrence reeled.

The cat began to lick Alice-Miranda's face. 'I think he's thirsty.'

'It must be travelling with someone,' Lucas looked around, but there was no sign of a vehicle anywhere and the view was clear for miles. 'It's got a collar.'

'Maybe it was separated from its owners?' Jacinta said, giving the affectionate moggy a rub on the head. 'And now it's lost.'

Millie retrieved a flask from the car and poured some water into the lid. The cat leapt down and began to lap it up as soon as she put the vessel on the ground.

'Weren't there some tins of salmon in that grocery order?' Hugh rummaged in the back of the Landcruiser until he found what he was after.

He pulled the lid off and placed the tin on the ground beside the water. The cat tucked in, finishing the fish off in less than two minutes.

'Poor thing – he must have been starving,' Alice-Miranda said.

'What now?' Lawrence asked. He looked at Hugh.

'Well, we can't leave the cat out here. He'll be prey for something,' the man said.

'Those pterodactyls will get him in a heart-beat,' Jacinta said seriously.

'Hmm,' Hugh bit his tongue and glared at Millie, willing one of the children to set the girl straight, but unwilling to spoil their fun.

'We've got to take him with us, Daddy,' Alice-Miranda said.

'Her,' Lucas corrected.

'How do you know that?' Millie asked.

The boy had knelt down to give the creature a scratch. 'Her name's Junie. Says so on her tag.'

'Junie!' Alice-Miranda gasped. 'That's the same name as Taipan Dan's cat. That's what Sprocket said.'

The others nodded.

'Sprocket said Dan's been gone for three months,' Millie said. 'Junie looks like she's pretty well fed. She can't have been on her own for that long.'

'Sprocket also said that Dan loved his cat more than anything in the world,' Jacinta added. 'Why would he leave her here?'

'Who knows?' Alice-Miranda said.

'We'll take her with us and we can drop her in Coober Pedy when we head home,' Hugh said.

He glanced back to the cat.

'She's gone,' Jacinta said, turning a circle to look for the feline.

'Um, no, but I think she's ready to leave.' Alice-Miranda pointed.

Standing on the driver's seat with her paws perched up on the steering wheel, Junie the ginger cat meowed for them all to hurry up.

Chapter 7

'Ridley One, keep your eyes peeled for a vehicle. Over,' Alice-Miranda said into the two-way handset.

'How's Junie?' Jacinta asked. 'Over.'

Since they'd set off again, the cat had prowled all the way around the car before making herself comfortable on Millie's headrest, her paws perched on the top of the girl's head. Junie was now purring so loudly it sounded as if there was a tiger on board.

'She owns the car,' Alice-Miranda replied. 'If she could drive, I'm certain she'd have kicked Daddy out of his seat. Over.'

'Cute,' Jacinta said. 'Over and out for now.'

They'd already driven thirty minutes from where Junie had been found, and so far there wasn't any sign of a vehicle. No tyre tracks, no evidence of a breakdown. Nothing.

'Do you think something bad could have happened to Taipan Dan?' Millie asked.

'Anything's possible out here,' Hugh said. 'I'll try to contact Sprocket once we get to Hope Springs and find out what else he knows. I think it might be time to involve the police too.'

Alice-Miranda and Millie agreed.

'I'm just glad that we came along or poor Junie might have ended up as pterodactyl food,' Millie said with a giggle.

'You're terrible. We're *all* terrible,' Hugh corrected himself. 'Which one of you is going to tell Jacinta the truth?'

'I will,' Alice-Miranda said.

Millie frowned. 'No, I'll do it. It's my fault. I started it.'

Hugh hit some corrugations on the road and Junie meowed loudly in objection. Millie protested too, given the cat had held onto her position by digging her claws into the top of the girl's head.

'Hey you.' Millie reached up and was given a nip for her trouble. 'Junie here might not be as friendly as we first thought.'

Hugh chuckled as he watched the antics in the rear-vision mirror.

'Daddy, there!' Alice-Miranda pointed. Her father braked gently and the car was swallowed in the cloud of dust.

As the air cleared, everyone else could see what Alice-Miranda had spotted. A white four-wheel drive ute. It was parked on an angle on the side of the road and the driver's door was open, as if whoever had left it there did so in a hurry. Behind the cab sat an empty dog cage, the rest of the tray covered by a black tarpaulin.

Lawrence pulled up beside Hugh and put the passenger window down. Hugh lowered his window too.

'What do you think?' Hugh asked his brother-in-law.

'Approach with caution,' the man replied, opening the car door and waving away a swarm of flies. 'Stay here, kids.'

'Do you think it's broken down?' Millie asked.

'Maybe,' Alice-Miranda said.

Hugh hopped out and pushed up the sleeves of his checked shirt. Together, the men advanced towards the vehicle, not knowing what to expect. Hugh hoped that whoever the car belonged to was just having a nap and wasn't good at parking, while Lawrence's mind had gone straight to a body slumped over the steering wheel – probably because he'd once played a spy and had acted in a spookily similar scene in a desert in the Middle East.

Lawrence peeked under the tarp and grabbed a shovel from the tray, then walked around to the driver's door. He held the tool aloft, not sure what he was planning to do with it, and looked into the cabin of the vehicle. To his great relief, it was empty. Lawrence dropped the shovel and he and Hugh both let go of the breaths they'd been holding.

'Okay, so no one's dead – but where's the driver?' Hugh said.

'Key's still in the ignition,' Lawrence said as he investigated the cabin. 'I'll see if it starts.'

He jumped into the seat and planted his foot on the clutch then turned the key. The engine fired straight away. Lawrence peered at the dashboard and wiped away a coating of red dust. 'Got three quarters of a tank of fuel.'

Hugh poked around on the passenger side. He opened the glove box, which was jammed with maps and old roadhouse receipts, and took a quick look in the cooler bag full of food that sat on the floor along with three large flasks of water.

Lawrence pulled down the sun visor on the driver's side – but it was bare.

'Anything?' Hugh asked. He'd given the children the nod to leave the Landcruisers while checking the tray of the ute, where he'd found two jerry cans of fuel under the black tarp along with the tools.

'No,' Lawrence replied.

Hugh glanced past the approaching children to where Millie remained in the car, the now-sleeping Junie still perched on her head. 'Our feline friend hasn't shown any interest,' Hugh said. 'You'd think she might have noticed if it was her beloved master's vehicle.'

'Sprocket didn't say anything about Taipan Dan having a dog and this ute's set up for one,' Lucas pointed out. The others all frowned.

'Perhaps it came with the vehicle,' Jacinta said. 'And he just hadn't bothered to take it off the back? Or maybe he used to have a dog.'

Anything was possible.

'Come on, we'd better get moving or Barnaby will send a search party,' Hugh said. He pulled the phone from his top pocket, but there was no reception. He'd call the police when the party arrived at Hope Springs. Hopefully they could send someone out to investigate the ute and see who it belonged to.

In the meantime, he took several photographs showing the car and the way it was situated. Unfortunately, he didn't realise that the registration plate was covered in a thick coating of dust and impossible to read.

'Daddy, don't you think we should take a quick look around?' Alice-Miranda said. 'What if the driver got out to have a toilet break and they've fallen over and hurt themselves or had some kind of medical emergency?'

Hugh nodded. His daughter was right. Aside from a few scrubby bushes and trees though, there weren't really too many places for a person to be concealed nearby.

Jacinta and Lucas headed off towards a stand of mulga trees on the western side of the road, while Alice-Miranda and her father headed east. Lawrence continued looking through the ute to see if he could find any identification.

Seconds later there was an ear-piercing scream.

'Daddy! It's Jacinta,' Alice-Miranda cried. She took off across the road towards the trees, her father and uncle in hot pursuit. Inside the Land-cruiser, Millie heard the shriek too.

'Sorry, puss.' She pushed Junie off the top of her head. The cat meowed loudly and sprung through the gap in the front seats to the dash-board. Millie opened the door and jumped out, hoping that Jacinta hadn't been bailed up by a snake – because if that was the case she was high-tailing it straight back to the car.

'Jacinta, calm down,' Lucas was saying as everyone reached the pair, his hands outstretched.

'What is it?' Lawrence asked, taking a step back. A second later he realised the girl's predicament.

Jacinta was pressed up against a mulga tree. In front of her, an agitated lizard hissed and stood up on its hind legs, flaring the frill around its neck.

'He's a beauty,' Hugh said, running his left hand through his thick dark hair and biting his lip, wondering what their next course of action should be.

Millie reached the group and stopped dead.

'Wow! That's not supposed to be here. Frill-necked lizards generally inhabit the far north of Australia, and we're in the middle. Although my guide book did say that on odd occasions they could be found in the desert regions, so I guess this guy is one of those rare exceptions. Its proper name is a Chlamydosaurus.'

'Maybe that's why he's so upset,' Alice-Miranda said.

'What? Because he's got a funny name?' Millie said.

'No, because he isn't where he's supposed to be,' Alice-Miranda replied.

The problem remained that Jacinta was still trapped between the lizard and the tree with no clear escape route. The lizard began hopping from one foot to the other and hissing even louder.

'Why didn't anyone tell me there were dinosaurs out here? I wouldn't have come on this stupid trip,' the girl whimpered.

'You're okay, Jacinta,' Lucas cooed. 'Just stay still.'

Hugh and Lawrence exchanged glances, wondering if the creature was dangerous.

Millie had a thought and quickly returned to the car to get her camera.

'We could distract it,' Alice-Miranda said. She raced back to the car after Millie, grabbing a half-eaten sausage roll from the bag in the front seat.

'They mostly eat insects and spiders – and sometimes the occasional small mammal and reptile,' Millie said as they stumbled back over the rise to the mulga trees. 'I don't know if he'll enjoy a sausage roll, but you can try.'

Jacinta was trembling and tears were now streaming down her cheeks.

The lizard was getting more and more agitated.

It rushed at the girl, hissing, then danced a short distance back again.

'Help!' Jacinta screamed.

Millie snapped shot after shot. 'These pictures are amazing,' she declared.

'I don't care about your stupid photos!' Jacinta shrieked. 'Just get it away from me!'

Alice-Miranda pulled a piece of meat from inside the pastry casing and threw it to the ground. Unfortunately, the mince landed too far away from the lizard to distract the creature from Jacinta.

'Here, give some to me,' Lucas said.

Alice-Miranda passed the boy a piece and he lobbed it over. This time the meat hit the top of the lizard's head and dropped down right in front of it.

'Good shot,' Hugh said.

The lizard looked left and right.

'No, it's there, you silly thing,' Lucas urged.

Finally the lizard's tongue shot out and it gulped the morsel.

'More, more,' Lucas urged.

Alice-Miranda passed over the rest of the sausage roll, which Lucas tore up and threw to the creature. The reptile's attention turned to the food around it, gobbling the meat down as Jacinta edged past, not half a metre away. She ran to Millie and began to sob with relief.

'You do know it's *just* a lizard,' Millie said, giving the girl a hug. 'And those pterodactyls are really eagles. I was only teasing.'

Jacinta shook her head. 'I don't believe you. You're just saying that. I've seen them with my own eyes.'

She made a run back to the Landcruiser and shouted for the others to hurry up as she threw herself inside the vehicle and pulled out her phone. The girl wanted to tell her mother about her terrifying encounter, except there was no reception.

'Stupid outback!' she spat. Jacinta hurled the device onto the seat and began to cry. She wished she'd stayed at home. At least there she didn't have to worry about dinosaurs and snakes and flies.

'We should get moving,' Hugh said. 'There's no sign of anyone except old Frilly here.'

The lizard finished the sausage roll and then, with its path clear, made a run straight up the tree. Obviously poor Jacinta had got between the creature and its home.

A swirly breeze sprung up as Alice-Miranda headed back to the car. A piece of paper blew towards her and she reached down to pick it up.

She unfurled it and took a closer look. The page was the colour of tea and one edge was ripped, as if half of it was missing. The words 'Hope Springs' were written in swirly script at the bottom. The rest of the paper was covered in a squiggle of lines, and perhaps something to indicate a boundary. An 'X' was marked in the corner.

'What have you got there?' Hugh asked.

Alice-Miranda frowned. 'It could be a map, I think – something to do with Hope Springs. I wonder how it got here.'

Hugh took the page and had a closer look. 'I'd say that was drawn a very long time ago. You can show Barnaby. See if he makes anything of it.'

The man passed the paper back to his daughter, who folded it and put it in her jeans pocket. Within a minute or so the group was ready to leave.

As Hugh pulled onto the road, Alice-Miranda turned to look back at the abandoned ute. She had a strange feeling about it. Hopefully the missing driver was okay and not lost somewhere in the great expanse of desert. No one could survive out there for too long – especially without food and water – and whoever owned that truck seemed to have left all their supplies behind.

Chapter 8

'An hour and a half later, the two Landcruisers rumbled across a cattle grid. A red-dirt encrusted sign announced that they'd arrived at Hope Springs Station.

'Finally!' Millie announced. Junie had resettled on the girl's lap and was purring contentedly.

'I'm afraid we still have a while until we'll reach the house,' Hugh said.

'How far is it?' Alice-Miranda asked.

'About fifty kilometres,' Hugh replied.

'That's got to be the longest driveway in the world, or close to it,' Millie rubbed her eyes. Travelling was exhausting, and about an hour ago it hadn't only been Junie who was fast asleep – Millie and Alice-Miranda had taken naps too. It was hard to stay awake with the warm sun beating in the window and the engine humming, although the road corrugations had shaken the girls from their slumber several times. They hadn't passed another car or seen any sign of whoever owned the white ute.

'Hope Barnaby has the kettle on,' Hugh said. 'I could murder a cup of tea.'

The trio travelled on in silence until they finally spotted a building in the distance. It was a typical Australian farmhouse, with a wide veranda, a pitched iron roof and an architectural elegance befitting something that had been built a long time ago. As they drew closer, the girls could see the house was surrounded by a wire fence enclosing a neat garden with beds of Sturt's Desert Peas, an old concrete birdbath and a wooden seat that sat beneath a shady tree in the front corner.

A tan-coloured dog began to bark from the top step.

'Oh, Daddy, it's lovely,' Alice-Miranda beamed at her father. 'And just what I imagined an outback station to look like.'

Junie stood up and stretched on the back seat, then pressed her face against the window as if she was taking a good look to see where they were.

Hugh drove over another cattle grid and veered left to the rear of the house, where there was a cluster of outbuildings. Lawrence pulled up behind him.

A man Alice-Miranda recognised as Barnaby Lewis hurried out of the back door and down the steps, followed by two children and the kelpie, which came running from the front of the house. The dog's tail batted back and forth and it gave another couple of short sharp barks before one of the children told it to stop. The animal had one of those happy faces that looked like it was very glad to have company.

Barnaby and Hugh shook hands before the man spotted Alice-Miranda. 'Well, just look at you, young lady. You're practically a teenager.'

'Not quite,' Alice-Miranda reached up to hug her honorary uncle and planted a kiss on his cheek. 'But I am turning eleven next birthday.'

Alice-Miranda introduced everyone else as they emerged from the vehicles.

Barnaby turned to the children beside him. 'This is Hayden, he'll soon be twelve, and Illaria, who's just turned ten.' The dog gave a bark. 'Oh, and that's Rusty.'

'Dad!' Illaria protested. 'That's not my name.'

'Sorry, sweetheart – this is Larry, and don't dare be silly enough to call her anything else, especially the beautiful name her mother and I gave her at birth,' Barnaby grinned.

'It's not beautiful, it's ridiculous,' the girl said.

'Oh, I think it's lovely,' Alice-Miranda said.

'You can have it if you like.' The girl rolled her eyes and smirked.

'I thought they must have been two boys,' Jacinta whispered to Lucas. He'd been thinking the same thing.

'Dad said you're a good rider,' Larry commented, looking at Alice-Miranda.

'That's very kind of him. I have a pony called Bonaparte, who is probably the naughtiest pony in the history of the world, but we have a lot of fun, and Millie's a *great* rider. She has a pony called Chops, who pretends to be slow and lazy, but he often beats me and Bony,' Alice-Miranda said.

'Just for the record, I hate horses,' Jacinta said, batting her hand to swat at the flies.

Lucas cast her a glare. 'Jacinta!' he chided.

'Well I do. They don't like me and I don't like them, which is fine. But I'm quite partial to four-wheel motorbikes, if you have any of those,' Jacinta said.

Hayden smiled. 'I feel a bit the same way and yes, we have a few four-wheelers, and two-wheelers as well.'

'That sounds like fun,' Jacinta said.

Barnaby opened the gate into the garden that surrounded the house. 'Let's get the kettle on,' he said.

'Good idea. And can I use your landline? I need to make a couple of calls,' Hugh said.

'Sure.' Barnaby was about to head up the back steps when he spotted Junie on the back seat of the Landcruiser. 'Why is there a ginger cat in your car?'

'Long story, best told over a brew,' Hugh said. 'But we should bring her inside if that's okay.'

Junie was now standing on the back seat, peering out at everyone.

'We used to have a cat called Simba,' Hayden said. 'Until last month when a brown snake got her under the front veranda. Dad even gave her the antivenene that we keep in the freezer in case any of us gets bitten. She just kept getting weaker and weaker though, and by the time Dad and I got her to the vet in Coober Pedy it was too late. Larry was heartbroken and Mum cried for a week, but I don't think she knows anyone noticed.'

Barnaby looked at his son kindly. Simba had been a real character and especially loved the girls. He shouldn't have used the antivenene on her – apart from the fact it wasn't for animals, it cost a fortune and wasn't easy to get – but Larry had been hysterical.

'I'm sorry,' Alice-Miranda said.

'Can we keep this cat, Dad?' Larry begged. 'Please. You promised we could get another one soon.'

'Steady on, sweetheart,' Barnaby said. 'We need to find out how she came to be here in the first place.'

Millie opened the car door to pick up Junie, but the cat jumped down onto the ground. Rusty loped towards her and for a few moments there was a tense standoff as the pair considered one another.

'This is going to be interesting. Rusty hated Simba,' Larry said.

'Only because she dug her claws into his nose whenever he got too close,' Hayden explained. 'He's still got the scars to prove it.'

Despite his previous bad experiences, Rusty put his head close to Junie's and – to everyone's surprise – the cat rewarded him with a lick on the snout before flicking her tail and stalking up the back steps to the door. If Alice-Miranda didn't know better, she would have sworn the cat sat there impatiently tapping her paw.

When Barnaby opened the back door, Junie was the first one inside. Rusty followed her, his tail wagging. The pair of them disappeared down the hallway past the large country kitchen.

Following the animals in, Larry put the kettle on while Barnaby pulled some mugs from the cupboard.

'Hayden can you organise some drinks?' the man said to his son. 'Oh, and the bathroom's down the hall if anyone needs it. Turn right into the other hallway and it's the last door on the left.'

'Is there still a phone in the study?' Hugh asked.

Barnaby nodded. 'Everything okay?'

'We're not sure. We went to visit Sprocket in town and he told us a half-baked story about some bloke called Taipan Dan going missing. Apparently Dan's place is locked up tight and he's gone, along with his cat, Junie, which is the name on the collar of that haughty creature you've just met.'

'We found her about two hours from town,' Alice-Miranda said. 'We couldn't just leave her there in the middle of nowhere.'

Jacinta sniffed. 'The pterodactyls would have eaten her quick smart.'

Hayden and Larry looked at one another, frowning. Lucas shook his head and pressed his finger to his lips.

'I'll tell you later,' he mouthed.

'Anyway, there was no sign of Dan,' Lawrence said. 'But half an hour on we came across a white Hilux abandoned on the side of the road. It had an esky full of food inside, jerry cans with diesel in the back and three quarters of a tank of fuel, as well as a whole lot of tools – shovels and the like. The engine fired first go. We had a bit of a look around but couldn't see anyone – and there weren't really too many places to hide.'

Barnaby's brow furrowed. 'I've come across a fair number of breakdowns over the years, but that seems odd.'

The others agreed.

'Yes, I thought I'd give Sprocket a call and see what else he knows – if I can get him to focus for more than a few seconds – and then I was going to report the ute to the police in Coober Pedy. Just in case they wanted to investigate,' Hugh said.

'Oh, and I found this on the road near the car.' Alice-Miranda pulled the ancient piece of paper with the squiggly lines out of her pocket and passed it to Barnaby. 'It has Hope Springs written on the bottom. Do you think it means anything?'

He studied the page. 'Looks like a map. Strange you found it blowing about in the middle of nowhere. There are lots of old records in the ledgers in my father's study that might help you figure it out.'

'Don't you mean *your* study, Dad,' Larry corrected the man.

Barnaby gave a sad laugh. 'Of course. I guess I still think of it as my father's even though he's been gone for a very long time. You're welcome to take a look and see if there's anything interesting among all the old books, Alice-Miranda. Perhaps the missing part is somewhere there.'

'May I take a look?' Hayden asked.

Barnaby passed him the paper while Hugh took his mug and walked down the hallway to make his calls.

'Maybe it's a treasure map?' the boy said. 'Molly says there's a legend of an opal reef somewhere on Hope Springs.'

'Really!' Millie exclaimed. 'Where?'

'Well, if we knew that we'd have found it by now,' Hayden said with a grin. 'And Mum and Dad would be rich and we could move to the city.'

'I don't think so,' Larry scoffed as she walked into the pantry. 'We're never moving to the city!'

'Molly's been telling that story for years, and another one about some thief who made off with a big bag of opals from Coober Pedy and hid it out here somewhere,' Barnaby said. 'I'm not sure that either of them is true. It's a bit like the legend of Lasseter's Reef – a supposedly massive gold deposit on the western edge of the MacDonnell Ranges. No one knows if it really exists. The idea of a reef of gold or opals, not just a seam, is pretty wild. But if you kids can find it, well, that would make life easier for sure.'

Millie and Alice-Miranda turned to look at one another, their eyes glinting. 'An outback mystery! Now that's intriguing,' Alice-Miranda said.

Larry returned with a large cake inside a dome, and set it on the table. 'Dad and I made this yesterday. It won't be anywhere near as good as Molly's, but we used her chocolate cake recipe and the batter tasted yummy.' Larry began to cut the confection, which was sprinkled with a fine layer of icing sugar. Alice-Miranda helped put the pieces onto plates and pass them around.

'So I gather the difference between a reef and a seam is that a reef is a huge wall of minerals and a seam is what we saw at Sprocket's place – just a line of colour through the rock face?' the girl asked. She'd been thinking about the difference since Barnaby had mentioned the words.

'You got it,' Barnaby said with a nod. 'I don't think anyone's ever found a reef of opals – it's an old wives' tale.'

Jacinta could think of something she definitely *didn't* want to find. 'You don't have any of those dinosaur lizards around here do you?' she said, then took a sip of her lemon cordial.

'What do you mean?' Hayden asked.

'You know, that Chlam-thing,' Jacinta said. 'What was it called again, Millie?'

'Chlamydosaurus,' the girl grinned. 'Also known as a frill-necked lizard.'

'It's not a lizard,' Jacinta said. 'It's a dinosaur and you can't tell me any different.'

'Why would you think that?' Larry asked.

Jacinta explained the trauma of her earlier encounter.

'Molly says they bring bad luck,' Hayden said. 'She lives here with Ralph and their family, but they're away on Sorry Business at the moment.'

'Dad told us,' Alice-Miranda said. 'Will they be back soon?'

'We hope so,' Larry took another bite of her cake then lowered her voice. 'Dad's a terrible cook – he burns everything. It's a wonder we haven't starved to death.' Fortunately her father and Lawrence were too deep in conversation at the other end of the table for Barnaby to notice the jibe.

'Why does Molly think frill-necks are bad luck?' Millie asked. She hadn't come across any information about that in her guide book.

'She's always telling us Dreaming stories, but the one about how the lizard got its frill makes her cranky,' Hayden said. 'She says they're greedy show-offs.'

'Well, the one we met was terrifying,' Jacinta shuddered.

'I don't remember ever seeing one out here,' Larry said. She looked at her father. 'Excuse me, Dad, have you ever seen a frill-necked lizard on Hope Springs?'

Barnaby shook his head. 'No, and don't talk to Molly about them.'

'That's what we just said,' Hayden added.

Alice-Miranda hopped up and headed down the hallway to the toilet, peering into the lounge room on the way.

'Oh my goodness!' she exclaimed. 'Everyone, come and take a look at this!'

There was a screech of chairs on floorboards as Larry led the others to the room.

In the middle of the threadbare Persian rug, Rusty was lying stretched out on his side, sound asleep.

'I think Junie's found herself a new best friend,' Alice-Miranda said.

The cat was perched on the dog's body busily giving Rusty a bath.

'Dad, we have to keep her,' Larry begged. 'They were made for each other.'

Barnaby chuckled. 'Well, that is one of the strangest things I've seen in a while.'

'Oh, they're too adorable for words,' Alice-Miranda said.

Jacinta and Lucas lingered at the back of the group. Jacinta smiled at the boy and he gave her a nudge. 'So cute,' Lucas said. 'Like you.'

Jacinta blushed as Lucas held her hand while no one was looking.

Millie ran to the kitchen to grab her camera from her backpack.

'Surely this has to win me the school photography competition,' she said, and snapped away.

Chapter 9

By the time the family and friends had finished their afternoon tea it was almost time to start dinner. Barnaby had planned a barbecue and Lawrence offered to do the cooking. It was the least he could do as a guest. That, and he'd had one ear on the children's earlier conversation about Barnaby's habit of burning everything. He liked his steaks medium-rare and it sounded like Barnaby was more a fan of charred-to-death.

After their discovery of Junie and Rusty's fledgling love affair, the children had been shown to their sleeping quarters. Lucas was in the second bed in Hayden's room, while the girls were shown to a sleep-out in an enclosed section of the back veranda, which held three sets of bunk beds and a couch as well as an ancient television set. Larry was moving out of her room for Hugh, and Lawrence had the guest bedroom.

They also had a good look through the house. It had a breezy wide screened veranda running all the way around, and was intersected by hallways that ran front to back, east and west, north and south. There were high ceilings with ornate plaster cornices, ceiling roses and antique light fittings. The timber flooring and joinery harked back to a different era, although it appeared that someone had installed a 'new' kitchen half a century ago, with a giant old-fashioned cooker in the middle of the original fireplace. The cupboards had been painted white and, even though it was old, the whole room was fresh and clean.

Now, Millie was out taking photographs in the garden with Lucas and Jacinta while Hayden played tour guide. Alice-Miranda had just brought her suitcase in from the car when she bumped into her father on his way to find Barnaby and Lawrence.

'Did you get hold of Sprocket, Daddy?' she asked.

Hugh shook his head. 'No, he didn't answer, but that's not unusual. I did speak to the police in Coober Pedy and they're going to send a car out tomorrow to have a look at that ute. They can't get there today. A nasty accident has blocked the highway and it's all hands on deck dealing with that.'

'Did you tell the police about Junie?' Alice-Miranda asked.

'Sure did,' her father replied. 'They said they'd go and check on Taipan Dan, but apparently he's quite the hermit. It's no surprise he and Sprocket are mates – they're both a trifle odd.'

'I wonder why Junie was out there in the bush? Sprocket said that she and Taipan Dan were inseparable. I don't like that she was all alone,' Alice-Miranda said. She hated to think that something bad might have happened to the man.

Her father could only nod in agreement. He found the situation perplexing too.

'I'm going to help Larry with dinner,' the girl called after her father as he headed down the hall to the screened veranda.

Larry walked out of the pantry with some potatoes. She plonked them on the bench and pulled a saucepan from a cupboard under the bench. Then she picked up a peeler.

'What would you like me to do?' Alice-Miranda asked.

'There's a lettuce in the fridge, and some tomatoes and a cucumber too,' Larry replied. 'Maybe you could throw them together in a salad?'

Alice-Miranda nodded and went to retrieve the items. 'Do you grow your own fruit and vegetables?'

'Mum and Molly have a garden at the side of the house, but we haven't been able to water too much lately. Since the bore's broken, we have to save what's left in the tanks for drinking and showers. You'll have to let everyone know that it's a three-minute limit and only once a day,' Larry explained.

'That's fine,' Alice-Miranda said, though she would have a quiet word to Jacinta, who was known to spend a questionable amount of time in the bathroom at school each morning.

101

Their housemistress, Mrs Clarkson, was always telling her to hurry up and stop wasting water.

Alice-Miranda asked where she could find a salad bowl and set about pulling the lettuce apart, washing the leaves in the sink. She cut the tomatoes and cucumbers and added them too.

'What's it like living out here, so far from a town?' Alice-Miranda asked. 'It must be hard to make friends.'

'I love it,' Larry said. 'It's really peaceful, and there's something about the size of everything. It gives you a sense of wonder, I suppose – that we're so small in the world. Not in a bad way, though. Wait until you see the stars tonight.'

Alice-Miranda smiled. Larry sounded like an old head on young shoulders.

'Lucas and I stared at the sky for an hour last night. It was one of the most magical things I've ever seen,' Alice-Miranda said. 'I can imagine it will be even better out here.'

'I'll see if Dad will let us bring Grandad's telescope out,' Larry said. 'As for friends, well, I know other kids from the School of the Air and every now and then we meet up in Coober Pedy or Alice Springs, but I don't mind really. We've got Molly's grandchildren, River and Storm, to play with. They're like our other younger brother and sister. Stormy is so clever and seriously, River's a cattle whisperer – the cows love him. He taught me how to hypnotise Molly's chooks too.'

'I'd love to see that,' Alice-Miranda said.

'We can try after dinner,' Larry said.

'Does Hayden enjoy it as much as you do?' the girl asked. She was hunting around in the pantry and found a tin of beetroot, which she opened and poured into a bowl.

Larry shook her head. 'No way. He can't wait to go to boarding school in Adelaide, and then he says after school he's going straight to uni and leaving for good. He wants to be a pilot and live in a high-rise apartment overlooking the beach. I couldn't think of anything worse. It would feel like a prison to me. I suppose the one good thing would be less snakes.'

'Are you going to boarding school too?' Alice-Miranda asked.

'Not if I have anything to say about it,' the girl replied, peeling the last potato before lighting the gas stovetop. 'Mum and Dad have booked me in, but I would much rather stay here.'

'You never know – you might like it,' Alice-Miranda said as she looked in the drawers for some cutlery. She began to set the long kitchen table. 'Millie and Jacinta and I all go together and we have a great time. I can't imagine being at a regular day school any more, though I know it's not for everyone. Some girls get terribly homesick, but we do our best to make everyone feel welcome.'

'We'll see,' Larry said, helping to put out some glasses. 'Maybe if Mum and Dad make me go, I could come and do an exchange at your school – the way Uncle Hugh did when he met Dad.'

'That sounds like a great plan,' Alice-Miranda said. She began to tell Larry all about Winchesterfield-Downsfordvale, and the teachers and other students, and the way Miss Grimm used to be miserable but now she was lots of fun and had a little girl called Agnes who everyone called Aggie. By the time the girl finished, Larry didn't seem nearly as averse to the idea of boarding school as she had been to start with.

The telephone rang.

'Can you keep an eye on the potatoes for me?' Larry asked, flinging the tea towel that had been over her shoulder onto the edge of a chair. She raced to answer the old handset on the wall inside the huge walk-in pantry.

The potatoes came to the boil and Alice-Miranda turned the gas down and let them simmer. Then she went to the fridge to find some butter to spread over the top of them when they were done. She closed the door and turned around as Larry walked back into the room, her face ashen.

'Is something the matter?' Alice-Miranda put the butter on the bench and hurried over to the girl.

'That was Laura – she and Cameron are our closest neighbours over at Darley's Creek. We share a boundary about one hundred kilometres to the east. Their four-year-old daughter, Matilda, is missing. Laura thought she was with Cameron and he thought she was with Laura, but they worked out she's likely been gone since early afternoon and one of their dogs is missing too.'

'That doesn't sound good,' Alice-Miranda said. She couldn't imagine being out there on her own. You'd be lost in no time. 'Can we help?'

'That's why Laura called. She wanted to know if Dad was home. We have a helicopter in the back shed and there's still an hour or so of light left,' Larry said.

'Go! I'll finish getting this ready,' Alice-Miranda said, just as Hayden and the other kids charged up the back steps and onto the veranda.

Larry rushed past them as they entered the kitchen.

'What's up with her?' Hayden asked, heading straight for the fridge to get some cold water for everyone.

'Emergency at your neighbours' place,' Alice-Miranda said, and told them what she knew.

Chapter 10

'We can't just sit here and do nothing,' Larry protested, while stabbing at a piece of perfectly cooked beef.

'Dad said that there was no point us going out and getting lost tonight too,' Hayden said.

'As if that would happen to me,' Larry rolled her eyes. 'I know every inch of Hope Springs.'

'No you don't,' her brother retorted. 'Dad says there are places he's never seen, and he's been here a lot longer than we have. Stop showing off.'

Larry poked her tongue out at her brother and her freckles turned a darker shade of red.

'Your father said that if Matilda's still missing in the morning, we'll make a plan and help with the search,' Lucas said as he picked up another sausage and put it on his plate.

Barnaby had taken the chopper – a four-seater R44 that was used for mustering – to try to spot Matilda. The man didn't like to fly much any more and, after a particularly close call he'd made sure never to mention to Evie, had paid for Molly's son, Buddy, to get his licence down in Adelaide a few years ago. Buddy was a gun pilot – not afraid of anything. He could mix it with the best of the chopper cowboys in the bush.

But this evening there had been no other choice. Barnaby couldn't squander the chance of finding little Matilda before nightfall. Hugh and Lawrence had volunteered to go as extra pairs of eyes, and Barnaby was glad they had. That made it easier to insist on Hayden and Larry staying back to look after their guests.

Now, the light was fading. Millie and Jacinta stood up to clear the plates. Lucas volunteered to do the washing up.

'You guys can come and stay anytime,' Hayden said with a grin. 'Do you want to play cards later?'

'That sounds good,' Alice-Miranda said, welcoming the distraction. Although she didn't know Matilda or her family, she was nonetheless worried about the girl. It was clear that everyone else was too.

Larry looked at the kitchen clock. It was almost six and her father should be back soon – he couldn't fly at night. Five minutes later she heard the whumping of the blades overhead and raced out to see the aircraft landing beside the hangar. The girl charged through the back gate and down the track, eager to see if her father's mission had been successful.

'Did you find her?' she yelled at her father as the engine wound down.

Barnaby shook his head. 'No, but we'll head out again at first light and yes, this time you can all come and help. We'll need to make a plan and everyone has to stick to it – I don't want to be sending a search party for the search party.'

The girl nodded. Despite her earlier bravado, she knew as well as anyone what a perilous place the outback could be. Just a few years ago a family had got stuck, and instead of staying with their bogged four-wheel drive they'd all headed in different directions looking for help. That had ended in a terrible tragedy. Molly was always warning the children about the dangers of going off unprepared – there were too many sad stories.

Alice-Miranda and Millie had followed Larry outside.

Hugh looked at his daughter and shook his head. Lawrence wore a similarly forlorn expression.

'We've saved you some dinner,' Millie said, trying to raise the mood.

Barnaby did his final checks, then pushed the chopper into the hangar. There was a solemn air hanging over the group as they trudged back to the house.

'You will find her, won't you?' Millie broke the silence.

'Course,' Barnaby said, but there was something unsettling in his voice.

'Will the police come tomorrow?' Alice-Miranda asked.

'Yes, it'll be all hands on deck,' Barnaby said. 'Looks like the bore will have to wait another day.'

The man sighed quietly. It had been easy to see from the chopper that both their small dams were now almost completely dry, and the open storage wells too. If he didn't get things fixed, and soon, there would be no water in the troughs for when they brought in the herd. He still didn't know how he was going to manage without Buddy. He'd rung several pilots he knew, but they were all booked solid for the next month.

He hadn't told Hugh and Lawrence, but tonight he'd almost put them down miles away from home. A light had come on on the dash. Barnaby had been sure it was a warning. But it had gone off again and he'd held his nerve. His heart had been pounding and his hands were still clammy.

Barnaby hoped that by some miracle Buddy and the family would appear overnight, but he knew that wasn't likely. It wasn't safe to drive outback roads after dark – the roadkill along the Stuart Highway was testament to that.

'Did Matilda take anything with her?' Alice-Miranda asked, jolting Barnaby back to the present.

'Cam said her backpack is missing along with her favourite drink bottle, her lunch box and some food from the pantry. We're all hoping that she and

Blue Dog are curled up under a bush somewhere sound asleep and tomorrow she'll wander home again,' Barnaby said. He'd been in contact with the girl's father over the radio.

'Do they think she ran away?' Millie asked.

'Laura and Matilda have recently been to Port Augusta to visit Laura's parents. Matilda hadn't wanted to leave, so there's the possibility that she thought she'd turn around and go back,' Barnaby said. 'Sometimes little ones get crazy ideas in their heads and it doesn't matter what you say, they won't be deterred from their quest.'

'I know someone like that,' Hugh said, grinning at his daughter. 'Booked herself into boarding school at the ripe old age of seven and one-quarter.'

'That was a bit different, Daddy,' Alice-Miranda said. 'Matilda's only four.'

'There's something else I don't think I've told you,' Larry said.

The others looked at the girl.

'Matilda's deaf,' she said.

Barnaby nodded. He well remembered Cam and Laura's anguish when the child had been diagnosed. Living out here without easy access to medical facilities meant lots of long treks to the

112

city between remote speech therapy sessions and praying that the girl became a candidate for a cochlear implant. It hadn't happened yet.

'So she won't be able to hear the helicopters or motorbikes or voices calling for her,' Alice-Miranda said. 'Can she speak at all?'

Larry shook her head. 'That's another reason why we need to find her as soon as we can.'

Chapter 11

No one in the house slept particularly well that night. Everyone was thinking about Matilda, alone in the desert with only Blue Dog for company. Before bedtime, Larry had found some photos from when the Darley's had come for lunch the previous year. There was a gorgeous picture of Matilda sitting on Molly's lap, all dimples and dark curls with a cheeky grin, and another of her with Larry and Hayden. Barnaby had told them more about the neighbouring properties too.

Darley's Plains covered about half a million acres directly to the east of Hope Springs, which was double that size. To the north of both landholdings was Saxby Downs, the biggest station in Australia at over five million acres. The three properties intersected at a place called Hope's Corner.

Hope Springs and Darley's Plains had been in the Lewis and Darley families respectively for generations, but Saxby Downs had been sold twelve months ago to a multinational corporation. Cam said he'd had a run in with the new owner on his northern boundary a few months ago where the fellow had accused him of diverting water from Saxby Downs bores to fill his tanks. Cam had been mortified at the thought and Barnaby had been angry about the accusation too. Everyone knew how precious water was out here, and the very idea that someone would steal it was almost akin to murder.

With so many thoughts running through her head, Alice-Miranda was awake just after five. She slipped down from the top bunk, landing gently on the bare floorboards. Jacinta and Millie were asleep, though they'd all been tossing and turning for hours. Larry's bed under hers was empty.

She tiptoed along the veranda, opened the screen door that led to the kitchen and padded down the hallway to the toilet. On her way back, she heard Larry talking. Alice-Miranda stood in the doorway of the lounge room and listened for a moment.

'We have to find her, Junie,' Larry said. 'I'm not sure how long you were lost out here, but people don't tend to do very well on their own – especially not little kids. They can't kill bush rats for their dinner like you or I could if we had to. River showed me how to get them – we cooked one up on a campfire – it didn't taste too bad, but I prefer emu, and goanna's not bad either.'

Alice-Miranda poked her head in. 'I thought I heard you.'

Larry was sitting on the sofa, stroking the ginger cat, who had continued to make herself right at home. Junie had staked out several beds last night before deciding that Larry's was her favourite. Rusty slept on the floor right beside them. The cat and her new companion had barely left one another's sides. It was the oddest thing. Alice-Miranda looked around the room and was surprised that the dog wasn't there.

'Rusty's gone for a pee,' Larry said. 'This one just came back. I heard her meowing at the screen door and let her out. It was only a few minutes before she let me know she was ready to come back in again. She's a bit bossy, but I kind of like that. Everyone knows where they stand.'

Alice-Miranda grinned. 'Yes, I think she's already wrapped everyone around her little paw. At least she's well trained.'

'Mum wouldn't have been happy if she did her business in the house,' Larry said.

There was a whimper at the door, and Larry jumped up and ran off down the hall to let Rusty back in too. The dog raced down the hallway, his claws tripping on the floor until he charged into the lounge room and he jumped straight up on the couch beside Junie. He licked her head while she licked his nose. It was the cutest thing. Alice-Miranda wondered what Taipan Dan would make of his cat's new-found love.

'Let's get some breakfast,' Larry said as she reappeared at the door. The girls walked to the kitchen to find Barnaby was dressed and filling the kettle.

'Morning, girls,' he said with a nod. 'How'd you sleep?'

'Badly,' Larry replied.

'Not much better for me, I'm afraid,' Alice-Miranda said. 'I suspect we've all been thinking about Matilda. Do you have a plan, Uncle Barnaby?'

'Sure do,' the man replied. He'd just got off the phone with Laura, who said Cam had scoured the home paddock until four, when he'd returned to the farmhouse for something to eat. Despite his protests, Laura had insisted he have a lie down before they set out again or he'd be no use to anyone. Barnaby had heard the tension in Laura's voice as she'd spoken and knew the woman was putting on a brave face. If it was Larry or Hayden out there, he'd have been desperate too.

'The police have arrived at Darley's Creek, including Laura's brother, Ted – he's in charge of the operation. They're sending a tracker from Alice Springs as well, but he won't be here until midday. Some experts down at Coober Pedy have done the maths on how far a four-year-old might walk in the time she's been gone, so the police have set a radius from the house and we'll work from there,' Barnaby explained.

'Can we take the bikes?' Larry asked.

Barnaby nodded. 'It'll take too long to get to the search area on horseback, so you can go two kids to a four-wheeler, and Lawrence said he'll ride the trail bike.'

'Are you and Dad taking the chopper again?' Alice-Miranda asked.

'Yeah.' Barnaby sighed. 'I'd prefer Buddy was here so I could help with the ground search, but I'm still not sure when they're coming back. I thought I'd have heard from Molly by now,' Barnaby said as he finished making his tea and set about buttering a slice of toast.

The girls got themselves some cereal and sat down at the long table. It wasn't long before the others were up. It was something of a mission to ensure that everyone was fully equipped and briefed. Lunches had to be made and water bottles filled. Hayden and Lucas helped Barnaby get the two-way radios sorted – every vehicle had to take one. Barnaby photocopied a map of the area they were going to search. They'd move in a grid pattern, up and down. He impressed upon them that they'd need to look extra hard around mulga trees and scrubby brush, in case Matilda had crawled underneath and fallen asleep. Jacinta was not impressed by that idea at all following yesterday's run in with the Chlamydosaurus, but she knew she had to deal with it. A little girl's life depended on them all being thorough.

The family and friends met at the machinery shed to be briefed by Barnaby again just as the sun began to rise. He also wanted to check that Lucas and Jacinta both knew how to manage the four-wheel motorbike, since they'd be operating their own. He gave them a quick lesson and then tested their skills. Both of the children had ridden the vehicles before and proved competent. With helmets issued, sunscreen checked (several times by Millie, who had been obsessing over the sun and getting more freckles) and arms and legs covered, the children and Lawrence mounted their metal steeds. They would head to the boundary between Hope Springs and Darley's Plains and start their search – of course keeping a look out for anything on the way. Just because the authorities in Coober Pedy had done the maths didn't mean Matilda couldn't have strayed further afield. She was a fit child, always out with her parents around the station and her mother said she could go all day like a wind-up toy. Their best chance was that

Blue Dog had stayed with her and would lead her home.

Jacinta turned the key and fired the ignition.

'Now, I don't want any of you speeding off,' Lawrence shouted over the pinging of the 250cc engines. 'If you see anything, radio in – and if you get into any trouble, radio in – and let's hope to goodness we find Matilda soon.'

The children nodded and Larry led the charge. Alice-Miranda was seated behind her, while Millie was with Hayden. Lawrence brought up the rear on a trail bike, and over in the hangar Barnaby and Hugh had just finished prepping the chopper. They'd had to refuel, and Barnaby wanted to do some final checks. Not ten minutes later, the helicopter rose into the sky, flying over the children and Lawrence, who gave them a wave.

As sunlight flooded the horizon, it felt as if it was going to be the warmest day since their arrival. And that didn't bode well for little Matilda.

'We'll find her,' Alice-Miranda yelled to Larry over the mosquito buzz of the four-wheeler. The girl grimaced. There was no other option. They had to.

Chapter 12

The man winched another bucket of rocks and soil to the surface, grabbed it from the hook and walked the twenty metres or so to dump it on the growing mullock pile. It had been eighty-five days since he started on this hole, and it finally looked as if all that hard work was about to pay off. Dan lowered the bucket back down before scaling the ladder after it. His skin prickled with sweat and dirt. He shone his headlamp against the wall and examined it through his magnified glasses.

'There!' He grabbed the pick and began to chip away. 'There's got to be something in that . . .'

Dan spent over an hour dislodging another piece of potch, jabbering to himself all the while and wondering where that damn cat had got to. Little minx had jumped out of the cabin and taken off after a bush rat when he'd stopped for a pee just over a week ago. It had been right on dark. He'd called and called and camped on the side of the road for the night, but in the morning there was still no sign of her. He couldn't just sit there for days – he had work to do. Maybe she'd find her way to the campsite – it was a long way but cats were known to travel. It was her own silly fault, though he missed her more than he'd ever confess. That blasted cat was the light of his life and without her he felt lost.

When the piece of rock finally came free, the man's shoulders slumped.

Nothing again, but he wasn't about to give up. There were too many promising leads.

Dan's stomach growled and he realised that he hadn't eaten for hours. It was no wonder he was feeling lightheaded. He was planning to drive to town tomorrow, and he'd look for Junie again.

Hopefully she hadn't turned feral yet. Though, if he knew that cat half as well as he thought he did, she probably had the eagles doing her bidding, supplying her with an endless feast of bush rats and sleeping in a hollow under the mulga trees.

It was annoying that he had to go back again after only a week, but it was his own stupid fault. Dan had procured food for months, but he'd clean forgotten to have his prescriptions filled and without his medication, he wouldn't last long.

Dan put his pick on the ground and made his way back to the ladder. He stepped onto the bottom rung and placed his hands on the sides then took one step and another until he was about halfway up and realised something didn't feel right. His head was spinning. He reached his left hand up to the next rung, but the metal disappeared before his eyes. Seconds later, the world tilted off its axis and Dan fell backwards, hitting his head against the wall of the shaft and falling to the floor.

★

Alice-Miranda held onto Larry's waist as the girl sped across the open plains. The children and Lawrence were riding four abreast to stay out of each other's choking dust. It had taken over an hour to reach the boundary of Hope Springs and Darley's Plains, and now they had to locate the gate which was a kilometre or so further north. On the way, they'd seen mobs of red kangaroos and emus and had a close call with a camel who had broken away from a herd and seemed to be practising its sidestepping skills, weaving in and out of the bikes to the surprise of the children.

Once they had crossed over into the neighbour's property, the group split up into their search areas, first heading closer to the homestead then riding up and down in straight lines, taking it slowly and keeping an eye out for any movement.

It was hot and tiring work requiring a huge amount of concentration. Alice-Miranda could taste the fine red dust that seemed to get into every orifice. When she took a moment to blow her nose, she realised the tissue was a horrible shade of brown.

After a couple of hours, Larry brought the four-wheeler to a halt and radioed the others.

'We're taking a break for a few minutes. Over,' the girl said.

Her brother and Lucas concurred, and Lawrence said he was having a short rest too.

Alice-Miranda hopped off the back of the bike and removed her helmet and goggles, which were covered in a thin smear of red earth. She took a clean tissue from her pocket and gave them a wipe before leaning up against the four-wheeler. Despite having been covered, her eyes still felt gritty. Larry pulled two water bottles from her backpack and passed one over, then snapped open the lid of a plastic lunch box and offered Alice-Miranda a large wedge of chocolate cake.

'I squirrelled this in for us. There wasn't enough for the others, so they have to make do with extra muesli bars,' the girl said with a smile.

'Thanks.' Alice-Miranda took the treat.

'I hate that there's been no sign of her yet,' Larry said. 'It's getting hot.' She could feel the perspiration trickling down the middle of her back.

Alice-Miranda nodded. 'At least they think she has some water with her, and food – that's something. Her parents must be out of their mind with worry. I know mine would be.'

The girls were quiet for a time as they ate their cake and sipped their water.

'How are you feeling about everything?' Alice-Miranda asked.

Larry looked up at the girl. 'Worried – same as everyone.'

'It must be hard with your mother away and your grandmother not well,' the child said.

Larry nodded. 'I wish Hayden and I could have gone to Sydney, but Mum insisted we stay and help Dad. I feel sorry for her having to deal with everything on her own. Dad said that Granny's been a bit difficult.'

'Dementia is a horrible thing,' Alice-Miranda said. 'I think Granny Bert is in the early stages too. She's not really my granny, even though she's been part of our family forever and lives on our property. It's sad to see her forgetting things and getting cross.'

'Granny kept calling me Evie the other night on the phone, and when I said I was Larry she said that was ridiculous – I sounded like a girl,' Larry rolled her eyes. 'I'm glad you're here. It's nice to have some company around the place. It's been quiet since Molly and her family left. I hope they come back soon so you can meet everyone. Stormy's totally fearless. And smart too – way smarter than me and she's only eight. She wants to be a doctor and I think she could do it. She's always reading Grandpa's old medical journals from the study and telling me Latin words I've never heard.'

'Was your grandfather a doctor?' Alice-Miranda asked.

'Yes, but he never practised, except bush medicine out here when workers on the property needed him. He delivered a few babies too. He wanted to leave Hope Springs, but something happened to his older brother. No one ever talks about Uncle Chester, but he's the reason Grandpa had to come home and run the station. I should be grateful about whatever it was because if Grandpa hadn't taken over, then the farm would probably have been sold and I wouldn't get to run it when I'm older. Dad doesn't talk about his father much – says he was a difficult man and he never knew his uncle at all. I suppose every family has their skeletons – that's what Mum says anyway.'

Alice-Miranda thought about the girl's words. 'I think that's true. There are always secrets. My dad has a brother he didn't know about until a few years ago. Daddy grew up thinking he was dead but we found him very much alive in New York. I love that they were reunited. Now Uncle Ed comes to visit and he and Daddy are really close. My dad's father was a difficult man too. He was heartbroken when my grandmother died in an accident and he seemed to take it out on his sons. I'm so fortunate to have the parents I do.'

'Yeah, me too,' Larry said.

Alice-Miranda noticed the worry line on the other girl's forehead. She reached out to touch her arm. 'Everything's going to be okay. I've got a good feeling.'

'Thanks,' Larry replied. 'Me too.'

There was crackle of static over the two-way radio and Millie's voice came through.

'Hey guys, Hayden and I think we've found something. Over,' the girl said.

Alice-Miranda picked up the handset that was sitting on the bike seat. 'What is it? Over.'

'Some crusts of bread under a mulga tree,' Millie replied. She gave the others their coordinates. Larry and Alice-Miranda hopped back onto the four-wheeler and started the engine. 'We're on our way.'

In the meantime, Lawrence radioed the location to the chopper too. So far, Barnaby and Hugh had covered a vast distance and seen nothing except cattle, roos and a huge herd of camels.

An hour later, the motorbikes descended on the spot where Millie and Hayden were waiting.

Alice-Miranda inspected the bread, which had stiffened in the dry air.

'I'm surprised a goanna hadn't found that,' Larry said.

'It's Vegemite, isn't it?' Alice-Miranda said as she gave the crust a sniff.

Jacinta screwed up her nose. 'Goannas probably hate that stuff as much as I do. That's why it's still here.'

'I've called it in to Laura. She said the tracker has just arrived from Alice Springs and he's on his way with Sergeant Johnson,' Lawrence said. 'But in the meantime we should fan out from here and see what we can find.'

'Sergeant Johnson is Laura's brother and Matilda's uncle,' Hayden said to the sweaty group.

'Wow, it's weird that the community out here in the middle of nowhere seems just as small as Winchesterfield – that's the village where we go to school. Everyone knows everyone and half of them are related,' Millie said. 'Myrtle Parker loves nothing more than to spread stories, although she has been slightly better behaved since her husband came out of his coma.'

Larry and Hayden raised their eyebrows at one another.

'Story for another time,' Alice-Miranda said.

'That happens out here too,' Larry said. 'But our town gossip isn't even in the closest town. Her name's Sharon, and she and her husband Wally . . .'

'Run the Kulgera Roadhouse,' Millie finished the girl's sentence.

'So you've had the pleasure?' Larry said.

'I wouldn't call it that,' Jacinta replied.

'Did she say terrible things?' Hayden asked.

'Only about one of Dad's movies.' Lucas grinned and his father arched his left eyebrow.

'I had to laugh,' Lawrence said. 'Otherwise I might have cried. I'm just glad she doesn't work for the *Hollywood Reporter*.'

'She has no filter,' Larry said. 'She's probably told everyone within a thousand kilometres that Mum's upped sticks and left Dad just because she's gone to Sydney to take care of Granny.'

'She has no decorating skills either,' Millie quipped. 'Seriously, who has a live snake on their shop counter?'

Alice-Miranda remembered Sharon's last words to them as they left the roadhouse. 'There was something odd,' she started. 'We were walking out the door and Sharon called out something like "It was Hope Springs you said you were headed, wasn't it?" And when I asked her why, she gave Wally this strange look as if she wanted to say something but thought better of it.'

'Probably ancient gossip,' Hayden said. 'Out here we call it the Bush Telegraph and Sharon is absolutely in charge of it.'

'Best she takes care of that than write film reviews,' Lawrence joked.

The group laughed.

'Should we get going?' Alice-Miranda suggested.

The others agreed. They had a quick check of their maps and worked out where they would focus their searches then zoomed away in different directions.

Chapter 13

Sprocket McGinty pulled up outside Taipan Dan's dugout. It had been months now since he'd seen his old mate, and he had a feeling in the soles of his leathery feet that something wasn't right. Sprocket let himself into the house the same as before. Nothing had changed, except there was a bit more stink coming from the kitchen. He wouldn't open the fridge – it was a potential health risk, and he didn't have the time to clean it out. Actually that wasn't true. He just didn't want to.

'Where are you, Dan?' Sprocket mumbled to himself. He'd come back figuring he'd take a better look around. Sprocket ferreted through some papers and a few envelopes on the dining table. Bills mostly – all unpaid too, by the looks of it. Nothing to indicate where his friend might have gone.

He walked down the hallway to the bedroom. Dan's bed was unmade. Sprocket tutted to himself and decided to tidy up. It wouldn't take a minute, and at least when Dan came back he'd have a nice made up bed to hop into, even if his fridge did smell. Sprocket pulled up the sheet and noticed something among the furl of bedclothes. It was a piece of paper – a photocopied note – not addressed to anyone, just words on a page. The text was faded and difficult to make out, especially since it was in a swirly, old-fashioned script. It was likely written some time ago, when people had cared more about good penmanship than they did today. Sprocket read the words aloud.

'The water on the table boasts a colourful feast, where Hope Springs eternal beneath a hungry rusty beast.'

He sat down on the end of the bed, the rhyme tumbling over and over in his mind. It was some sort of riddle. He'd enjoyed riddles as a kid, but they weren't something he'd had a crack at for a long time.

Sprocket had just folded the page when he heard the familiar clatter of a diesel engine. It didn't sound exactly like Dan's ancient ute – his had something of a D-minor arrangement and this engine was more B major, but perhaps Dan had got the old banger fixed. It had to be him, Sprocket thought. No one else ever visited. Dan kept to himself – it was something of a wonder they'd become friends, and that was really only because of a shared affinity for dynamite. At least now Sprocket could stop worrying.

The man walked into the hallway just as the front door opened.

'Where is it, you mongrel?' an angry voice growled. Sprocket froze. That wasn't Dan.

He looked left and right and thought about hiding behind the nearest door before remembering that dugouts never had any. Instead, Sprocket scurried back to the bedroom and ducked down beside the bed. He held his breath – his mind racing. He didn't know this voice, but whoever it was sounded like they were on a mission.

A crash echoed from the kitchen. Sprocket could hear cupboards opening and closing and things being tossed about. He heard the fridge door open. 'You filthy animal!' the intruder, who Sprocket presumed had just been overwhelmed by the rancid smell, declared.

The fridge door slammed shut and the trespasser moved into the lounge room, where Sprocket could hear furniture being thrown around and turned over. His heart was pounding. There was nowhere to hide and no other way out.

Then he had an idea.

Sprocket quickly messed up the bed again. He wrapped himself in the sheets and blankets, hoping that he'd blend into the bedclothes. It was a good thing he was so skinny, but until the guy left, he couldn't afford to move a muscle. He pulled the blanket over his head.

It wasn't more than a few minutes until he could sense the man's presence in the bedroom. The fellow was a heavy breather, and the physical activity had taken its toll – he was puffing and blowing and cursing under his breath. Sprocket almost yelped when the man sat down on the end of the bed. This was a disaster. What if the stranger decided to have a sleep? Sprocket had to keep calm or he'd give himself away. There was this one time, years ago, when he'd tried meditation. The voice in his head spoke to him.

Imagine a peaceful place – by a lake, near the ocean, in a field – anywhere calming. Slow your racing heart . . . He could feel it working – for a moment anyway, until the intruder spoke again.

'Where is it, Dan? It has to be here somewhere, you miserable old sod,' the fellow's voice was composed this time.

Sprocket felt the intruder stand up and then heard him moving around the room and towards the wardrobe on the far side. Sprocket opened his eyes and realised he could see through a tiny gap in the covers. He just hoped that the bloke didn't notice, or he was a goner. This fellow didn't sound as though he'd be inclined to sit down and have a cup of tea and a chat about what it was he was after.

As Sprocket watched, the man bent down to the floor and picked something up. 'What's this then?' Sprocket could almost feel the fellow's ragged breath. He cringed inwardly when he realised he must have dropped the paper he'd found on the floor.

There was silence for a few seconds before the man roared. 'You beauty! Now I just have to get my map from those thieving brats headed to Hope Springs.'

Sprocket flinched. Hope Springs – that's where Hugh and his mob had been off to. They didn't need this bloke paying them a visit. What sort of map was he after?

Sprocket continued his game of statues, willing the fellow to hurry up and disappear. Thankfully, the intruder soon walked back out of the room and down the hallway. The front door slammed. Sprocket was in the clear. He kicked off the covers and rolled onto the floor, hitting the ground hard. 'Ow!' he complained, then rubbed his nose and stood up.

'Hope Springs! I've got to get there before he does, or Hugh with Two and the rest of them are in trouble!' Sprocket said loudly. He ran out the front door without thinking, slamming straight into the burly brute.

'G'day, mate, whaddaya know?' the man said before he punched Sprocket in the face, knocking him out cold.

Chapter 14

The young man lifted his hat and wiped the back of his arm across his sweaty forehead.

'How much longer do you reckon this is gonna take, Muz?' he said. 'It'd be much quicker if we just capped them.'

'Course it would, and then it would be so much easier to trace too, you moron.' Muz – a stringy character with teeth like tombstones and a shock of bright orange hair – bit his lip.

Muz and Col had been out here for a while now. It was a big job. But so was the outback, everything about it was vast – the land, the sky, the distances, the problems. The boss at Saxby Downs had made their mission very clear. Leave no trail. They had to build up the pressure – if the station was going to double their herd in the next twelve months, they needed all the water they could get.

'Suppose at least while we're out here, our bank accounts are gettin' bigger. Nothing to spend it on,' Col said. 'Although I have something in mind next time we head to town. What do you reckon about a fire-breathing dragon right down the centre of my back – to complement the frill-necked lizard on my arm.'

'Is that what that thing is?' Muz said.

'Get out, the lizard's brilliant,' Col scoffed.

'Well, it sounds painful and expensive,' Muz said. 'I'd rather use my money to buy a patch of land so I can stop doin' other people's bidding.'

'Nah, we're young fellas. Don't wanna get tied down at our age. We should see the world – have some adventures,' Col said.

'Not me,' Muz shook his head. 'I'm gonna buy

a patch of dirt and some cattle and ask Elsie to marry me.'

Col shuddered at the thought. 'You'll have half a dozen kids in no time flat and never a second to yourself. I can't think of anything worse.'

'Well, that's just how we're different, Col. I want to get married and have a family and you want to get tattoos and travel. To each their own,' Muz said as he clamped two pieces of pipe together, then tightened the coupling. They needed more hardware – hopefully the boss had that sorted and would have it dropped in tomorrow. Earlier in the day, the men had seen a helicopter in the distance and ducked in under some brush for cover. They weren't taking any chances if it wasn't the boss and, as it turned out – it hadn't been.

The pair continued working until they were hampered by a lack of light. It would take an hour or so to get back to their bush camp, where it sat protected between some rocky outcrops. They even had water on tap, provided by the ancient windmill. The last thing they needed was for someone to find them – because if that was the case, there'd be no travelling the world or having families. Both were pretty tricky things to do from prison.

Chapter 15

It was five thirty when Barnaby radioed through to the kids that they were calling it a day. After the promising find of the Vegemite crusts, there had been nothing. Not a single clue.

The police had covered miles to the north and east of the property, while the children and Lawrence had scoured the west and part of the south. Barnaby and Hugh had been flying for hours and, apart from being exhausted, they were almost out of fuel.

'I feel sick,' Millie shouted to Hayden above the motor bike's engine as they rode towards Hope Springs.

The boy turned his head and looked at his passenger. 'I can stop if you need to.'

Millie shook her head. 'I just meant that I feel sick about not finding Matilda. How long can she survive out here?' The girl blinked back the tears that had been threatening for the past hour or so.

Hayden gave her a grin. 'She'll be okay. Kids are tough in the outback.'

Millie could only hope so. She hung on as they sped across the dusty plains towards the homestead, Hayden dodging yet another errant camel, who seemed to come from nowhere.

It was fair to say that the rest of the party were feeling much the same. Leaving the search without having found Matilda had given everyone an awful sense of foreboding. They should have found her by now, surely.

This was open country peppered with clumps of bush and mulga trees. She was a four-year-old. She couldn't have travelled that far.

Over at Darley's Plains the police had radioed to say they would continue their search into the night for as long as they could – then they'd camp where they were and resume first thing in the morning. Laura had stayed at the house, manning the radio and praying that her little girl would magically show up. She was doing her best not to panic, but it was getting harder and harder as every hour ticked by. What if Matilda had been bitten by a snake? What if she'd stumbled into one of the wells? What if she'd fallen asleep in the sun? Laura felt as if she might go mad with worry. Her parents were on their way from Port Augusta and due any time now. At least when they arrived she'd have someone other than herself to talk to.

It was right on dusk when Alice-Miranda and Larry arrived home. They were the first back, but the others couldn't be too far behind.

Alice-Miranda pulled off her helmet and ran her hand through her sweat-soaked hair. 'I thought we'd find Matilda for sure after Millie and Hayden located that crust.'

Larry nodded. 'Me too. It's as if she just vanished.'

'Should we put the bike away?' Alice-Miranda asked.

'I'll do it,' Larry said. 'You can get us some

drinks. There's plenty of ice in the freezer and lime cordial in the pantry.'

Alice-Miranda walked up the steps while Larry jumped back onto the four-wheeler and turned the engine over, steering the vehicle towards the machinery shed.

'Hello you two,' the child said, as she opened the screen door and was greeted by Rusty and Junie. 'You haven't done anything smelly in the house, have you?' She realised they'd been locked in all day and were probably desperate to go to the loo.

Junie and Rusty raced outside – the dog cocking his leg on the tree near the back gate while the cat padded out to sniff the garden before digging herself a hole and settling in to do her business in a more demure feline fashion. As Alice-Miranda was about to head inside, she thought she heard the distant sound of an engine being carried on the breeze that had sprung up earlier.

She stopped, then wandered around the side of the house. Way off in the distance, she could see a vehicle with a trail of dust behind it. Perhaps it was one of the police officers, although she'd thought they were all to the east of Darley's Plains.

She remembered the binoculars in her pack and ran back inside to get them, then charged out to the front veranda and quickly fiddled with the focus. The car was a white ute, and she was pretty sure that it had a dog cage on the back, although it was a long way in the distance so she couldn't be sure. If it was the same car they'd seen on the way out, though, it was a relief to think the driver had been reunited with their vehicle. She'd tell the others as soon as they returned.

Chapter 16

Red dust billowed up behind the ute as the young men covered the fifty or so kilometres back to their bush camp. Finally, they approached the rocky outcrop and Col eased off the accelerator, bringing the vehicle to a juddering stop under the cover of some scrubby trees.

'You're cooking tonight,' Col said as they hopped out of the car. 'I drove.'

'Yeah, I know.' Muz lifted the esky from the tray and walked into camp. It was a basic affair, comprised only of a tarp strung between some mulga trees, a fold-up table, two chairs and a gas stove.

The pair had a routine. Whoever had driven home got to have a bush bath while the other man cooked. After dinner, the chef had a wash and the other bloke did the dishes. So far, there had been few arguments.

Half an hour later, the two men were sitting in their camp chairs, feasting on tinned beef stew and crispbread biscuits.

'Geez, Muz, I don't know what you've done with this tonight, but it's good,' Col said as he shovelled another mouthful.

'Thought I'd mix things up a bit, so I added a tin of beans,' Muz replied.

'Well, it's a darn sight better than that grilled Spam you served up a couple of nights ago,' Col replied.

Muz nodded and stood up to boil the billy for some tea. Suddenly, a loud snap and rustling of leaves sounded from the scrub. Muz spun around, his heart quickening, while Col put his plate on the ground and jumped to his feet. He ran to get the rifle from the ute on the other side of the clearing. You couldn't be too careful with the feral animals out here.

Col pointed the gun in the direction of the noise and together they watched and waited.

A blue cattle dog burst from the undergrowth, tail wagging as it sniffed everything in its path.

The men breathed a huge sigh of relief and Col put the gun down.

'Where the heck did you come from?' he said, but the dog ignored the sound of his voice, clearly on a mission to find something tasty.

Muz shook his head, relaxing as he watched the canine. 'Last thing we need is some farmer's stray mutt out here. I'm not feedin' him,' Muz said. 'Though you seem to be.'

Col shouted. 'Get out, you mongrel!' The dog had just located his dinner plate on the ground beside the chair. The pooch growled when he tried to shoo it away.

Col held up his hands. 'Okay, it's yours. But I hope there's some more in the pot for me.'

'There is,' Muz replied, 'but I have a feeling we might have to give that to someone else.'

'What are you talking about?' Col asked.

Muz pointed towards the bush.

Col's jaw just about hit the ground as he spotted the girl, all brunette curls and dimples, standing in the clearing. She wore denim overalls and a long-sleeved T-shirt, and was carrying a small green backpack. 'Where on earth did you come from?' he gasped.

The little girl didn't say a word.

'What's your name, kid?' Col asked.

But the child didn't reply. Instead, she licked her lips and put the backpack on the ground before pulling out a drink bottle and opening the lid. It was empty.

'Get her something, will you,' Col urged.

Muz fluffed around for a few minutes until he found a flask of drinking water, sniffing to check its freshness. He passed it to the child, who grabbed it and drank greedily.

'Do you want something to eat?' Muz asked, but the girl still didn't reply. Frowning, Muz mimed the act of eating. The child nodded. 'I think she's hungry.'

'Congratulations, Einstein,' Col said.

Muz produced a clean plate from the box on the back of the ute and scooped some stew onto it then grabbed a fork – wiping the latter with the bottom of his shirt. He motioned for the child to sit in one of the camp chairs and passed her the food. The little girl tucked in while the two men stared from her, to one another and back again.

'Where did she come from?' Col said, shaking his head.

'Maybe she ran away from a car – we did see those tyre tracks last night,' Muz said.

'Has to be someone else camped out here,' Col said. 'It's at least forty clicks to the nearest homestead.'

'What if that helicopter we saw was looking for her?' Muz said. 'What are we going to do?'

'We can't call it in,' Col said. 'The coppers will come out, and then they'll want to know what we're doing here.'

Muz turned to her. 'Sweetheart, where do you live?'

The girl didn't look up, her gaze firmly on the plate. The dog, having finished Col's dinner, walked over to sit at the child's feet.

'Kid, what are you doing out here?' Col tried. His patience was starting to wear thin. 'Where's home?' he boomed loudly, but she still didn't flinch. 'What's wrong with her?' Col said.

Muz crouched in front of the girl and her dog, the canine watching his every move.

'Sweetheart, can you hear me?' he asked slowly. 'Would you like some ice-cream with chocolate sauce and sprinkles on top?'

'Well, that's mean, gettin' the kid's hopes up like that. Unless you have a magical ice-cream maker stuffed up your shirt,' Col scoffed.

Muz stood up and turned to his mate.

'She's deaf,' he said. 'She didn't hear a word I said.'

'Oh geez,' Col sighed. 'Her parents must be worried sick.'

'What are we gonna do?' Muz bit his lip.

'I dunno, but we can't keep her,' Col said.

'Well, we'd better think of something, and fast.'

Muz sat down on the spare chair and rested his head in his hands. The girl hopped up from her seat. She walked over and leaned against him. Her eyes began to close and she started to wobble. Fortunately, Muz grabbed her before she fell – the poor little darling was quite literally asleep on her feet.

Chapter 17

Sprocket McGinty opened his eyes. His head was pounding. He licked the top of his lip, which tasted like blood.

That punch had knocked him out cold. Now, he had no idea where he was, although given the roar of the engine and the grooves in his back, he guessed he was in the back of that bloke's ute. It was pitch black and airless with the tarp pulled tight over the tray. He had no idea how long they'd been travelling.

The engine slowed for a moment and Sprocket began planning his escape, except he realised there was no point until he knew where they were and how he might find help. Leaping from a perfectly good vehicle into the middle of the Australian outback could turn out to be a very bad decision.

He could hear a country tune playing in the cabin, and every now and then the driver would sing the chorus with a voice that could cut glass.

Sprocket wished he'd got a better look at the bloke, but the only thing he'd almost seen coming was the knuckle sandwich and by then it was too late.

The rhyme from the page he'd found played around and around in his head.

The water on the table boasts a colourful feast, where Hope Springs eternal beneath a hungry rusty beast.

What did it mean? The intruder had said something about a map. A map of what? What was he looking for? Water on a table. A rusty beast. Could that be an old car? A tractor? Sprocket had plenty of rusty beasts at his own place. Did 'Hope Springs eternal' mean whatever the man was looking for was at Hope Springs? That seemed to make the most sense, which was a worry. Hugh and the kids were out there and this bloke had already proven himself to be dangerous.

★

By half past six, the entire search party had arrived back at the homestead. It had been a long day, and everyone was hungry and keen to wash off the day's grime. Faces were speckled with red dust and Millie dug an impressive pile of dirt from her grit-encrusted ears just by running her finger around the inside.

Unlike the rest of the dishevelled bunch, Lawrence still looked every inch the movie star. He tousled his dark hair and, ridiculously, it fell into place – even though he'd worn a helmet most of the day.

Millie nudged Alice-Miranda. 'How is that possible?' She gestured at the man.

Alice-Miranda frowned. 'What are you talking about?'

'How does Lawrence look as if he's just stepped from the pages of an outback advertisement when the rest of us appear to have been dragged backwards through a mulga bush and jumped on by a cranky kangaroo?'

Alice-Miranda grinned. 'Must be the movie star gene.'

Jacinta had cottoned onto the conversation too. 'I know – just look at him,' she said with a sigh, staring at Lucas, who was almost as remarkably fresh as his father.

Millie shook her head.

'What?' Jacinta asked.

'We were talking about Lawrence, not Lucas,' the girl replied.

'Oh, I knew that,' Jacinta rolled her eyes.

'Sure you did,' Millie teased and gave her friend a nudge.

'I'm starving,' Larry said. 'Is there anything for tea?'

Hugh nodded. 'How do tinned spaghetti jaffles with cheese sound?'

Alice-Miranda smiled. Jaffles were a treat her father made sometimes when Mrs Oliver had the night off. The whole family loved them – including Mrs Shillingsworth, their live-in housekeeper – though they all agreed not to tell Dolly. The family cook thought the dish was a dreadful affront to culinary sensibilities.

'Delicious,' Larry said. 'As long as it's not Dad's chargrilled meat and three serves of soggy veg, I'm happy.'

'Thank heavens you're here, Hugh – otherwise my children were in danger of being starved to death.' Barnaby grinned.

'Oh,' Alice-Miranda said suddenly. 'I heard a vehicle before you all got back. I took the binoculars and had a look, and I think it was a white ute, possibly with a dog cage on the back.'

'Which direction was it heading?' Barnaby asked.

The girl explained that she'd watched from the front veranda. The car seemed to be travelling north almost parallel to the driveway, but further away.

The man's forehead puckered. 'Mmm, I wonder where on earth they were going, though if it was the ute you saw on the way out here, at least that's one less mystery for the police to solve.'

The children nodded.

'Why don't you all get cleaned up before dinner?' Hugh suggested. 'It'll take a little while.'

'A shower would be heaven,' Alice-Miranda said.

'Only if you like the sprint version,' Jacinta quipped. 'I hardly have time to get wet before the buzzer goes off. I mean, how am I meant to wash my hair?' She tugged at her matted blonde ponytail.

'Never mind, Jacinta,' Lawrence said. 'We should all be doing our bit to conserve water, no matter where we live.'

'Dad's right,' Lucas said. 'It's only coming out here you realise just how precious it really is.'

'It's okay for you two,' Jacinta said. 'You could go for a week without a bath and still look beautiful. But I suppose you've got a point,' the girl conceded.

Barnaby finished making cups of tea for himself, Hugh and Lawrence, and carried them over to the table. 'I need to get that bore fixed or we'll be dry before the end of the week.'

Everyone was silent a minute, knowing the increasingly desperate search for Matilda was the reason repairs were delayed.

'Did Laura say anything more, Dad?' Hayden asked.

'No, not much,' the man replied. 'She sounded exhausted.'

The enormity of the situation seemed to hit everyone at the same time. Barnaby looked at the sea of hangdog faces.

'Chin up, everyone. Matilda's a tough little nut,' Barnaby said. He knew that was true, but he also knew the reality of this land. He couldn't help feeling sick about the situation.

There were nods all round. 'Tomorrow,' Millie said. 'Tomorrow we'll find her.'

The others all agreed.

Chapter 18

'Where are you gonna leave her?' Col whispered, as he rolled the ute to a slow halt, keeping the machinery shed between the car and the darkened house.

'I'll find somewhere safe,' Muz replied softly. The tiny girl nestled in his lap began to stir, opening her eyes for just a second before promptly closing them again.

The two men had driven over fifty kilometres to the closest homestead, creeping the vehicle along the last ten kilometres as quietly as possible, guided only by the moonlight. They'd left the dog tied up back at the camp. They couldn't risk the mongrel barking.

'Well, are you gonna help me or not?' Muz mumbled.

Col realised what the other man was asking and hopped out to open the passenger door, his feet crunching on the gravel.

Muz passed the child to Col.

'She's a sweetie,' Muz whispered. 'I hope I have a daughter one day.'

Col grinned. Even he had to admit that the kid was cute. It was a mystery how on earth she'd managed to find her way to their camp, but at least she'd come across them before anything horrible had happened. It was rough country out here, and Col shuddered to think of the dangers for a kid that size.

Muz hopped out of the ute and walked around to the open side of the shed. Between the four-wheelers and farm machinery were plenty of spots they could place the child. He spread a blanket on the floor, then motioned for Col to lay her down. Once on the floor, the girl rolled over and put her thumb in her mouth.

'Sleep tight, little one. You're home now,' Muz said. He wasn't entirely sure that this was where she lived, but someone would look after her. 'We'll get your dog back when we can — she'll be fine.'

And with that, he headed off, leaving the child sound asleep.

Alice-Miranda woke with a start. She'd been in the middle of the most vivid dream when she thought she heard an engine fire up. She glanced at the old digital clock on the bedside table between the bunks. It was three in the morning, too early for any search parties — she must have dreamt the noise.

Everyone was asleep, including Junie on the end of Larry's bed and Rusty stretched out in the middle of the old rug on the floor.

Alice-Miranda rubbed her eyes and lay listening to the night sounds. There it was again — the low grumble of an engine. Was she imagining it or not?

She swung her feet to the ground and made her way to the kitchen. The girl peered through the back windows and saw a glint of metal in the moonlight near the machinery shed. She decided to take a closer look. Alice-Miranda grabbed the torch that was hanging from the coat rack on the covered veranda and found her shoes by the back door. She checked them for critters first then shoved her feet inside.

Rusty had heard her rattling about and came to investigate.

'Come on, boy,' Alice-Miranda whispered. They set off through the screen door and down the back steps to the yard. The creaky gate threatened to wake the rest of the house, but thankfully when the girl looked back, the place was still in darkness.

She and Rusty walked around the first double garage towards the cluster of outbuildings to the rear and western side of the homestead. They had myriad uses, from car parking to machinery. The hangar for the chopper was the furthest away, and some other sheds were full of feed and equipment for the stock. Another dwelling with its own garden patch sat about a hundred metres to the west of the farmhouse. Molly and Ralph lived there with Rosie, Sam and the children.

A row of old stockman's dongas – single rooms where the jackaroos and jillaroos who used to come for the mustering would stay – created a border between the sheds and the domestic buildings. These days, they were only used a couple of times a year at most for an overflow of family and friends, save for the one used permanently by Buddy. Barnaby had mentioned that Evie was thinking about turning them into holiday accommodation for travellers keen for a slice of life in the Aussie outback. She had friends on other stations who'd done the same.

Alice-Miranda and Rusty turned the corner of the machinery shed to find nothing there. She must have dreamt the noise after all. For a moment, she stood still, peering into the darkness up past the hangar towards the paddocks, when she suddenly heard the sound again. This time she was sure it was an engine.

Rusty looked up at her and whimpered.

'You heard it too, didn't you, boy?' Alice-Miranda patted the kelpie's head.

She shone the torch onto the ground in front of her. There were fresh tyre tracks and footprints in the dust.

Rusty raised his nose in the air then darted away towards the machinery shed.

'Here, boy,' Alice-Miranda called, and started after him. 'What have you got there?'

The dog stopped and lay down near what Alice-Miranda thought was a pile of old chaff bags. But as she got closer, her breath caught in her throat. She raced over.

'Matilda!' the girl shouted.

Alice-Miranda knelt down beside the child and listened for breaths. Matilda was alive and fast asleep.

A happy tingle ran down Alice-Miranda's spine. 'You are going to make everyone very happy, little one.'

She wondered what to do – wake Matilda or leave her sleeping. The last thing she wanted was to scare the poor child half to death, especially as they'd never met before.

'Rusty, stay here,' she said. 'I'll be back in a minute.'

And with that Alice-Miranda took off. She ran up the back steps of the homestead, making as much noise as she could. Hopefully that would get them all up.

'Uncle Barnaby!' Alice-Miranda called as she ran inside. Junie was the first one out. The cat ran into the hallway, then stretched down on her front paws and arched her back. Seconds later, Hugh appeared, Barnaby and Hayden close behind him.

'What's the matter?' the man asked. 'What's happened?'

'I've found her. Matilda. She's asleep in the machinery shed,' the girl said. Everyone was up now.

'What? How on earth did you think to look there – and at this time of night?' Barnaby said, his brow creasing.

Alice-Miranda explained that she'd thought she heard a noise so she and Rusty went out for a walk. It was Rusty who deserved all the credit.

There were cheers and hugs as the girls arrived in the hallway too.

'Well, what are we waiting for?' Millie said.

'I think Uncle Barnaby and Hayden and Larry should go. We don't want to frighten the girl,' Alice-Miranda said.

Barnaby nodded. 'You're quite right. Hugh, can you call Darley's Plains and let Laura know? We'll go and get her. Come on, Alice-Miranda, you'd better lead the way.'

The girl flew back outside, with Larry next to her and Barnaby and Hayden bringing up the rear. When they reached the machinery shed, their smiles couldn't have been any bigger. Rusty had laid next to Matilda with his snout nuzzled against her hair.

'Oh, thank heavens,' Barnaby said as he knelt down. He gently touched Matilda's cheek and waited as she began to rouse and her eyes fluttered open. It didn't take more than a few seconds for her to register the familiar face. She reached out her arms and began to cry. Barnaby held her tightly, tears streaming down his own cheeks. Behind him, the other three children were crying too.

'This is the best news,' Larry said, turning and giving Alice-Miranda a tight hug. 'I don't think I've ever felt more relieved.'

'Me either,' Hayden agreed, wrapping his arms around both girls.

Barnaby scooped Matilda up and noticed the blanket she was lying on.

'Where did this come from?' he said.

'I think someone put her here,' Alice-Miranda said, explaining more about the engine noise she thought she'd heard and the fresh tyre tracks.

'But why would they do that? They could have brought her straight to the house,' Hayden said. 'And where did they find her?'

'Is she hurt?' Larry asked.

Barnaby prised Matilda's arms from his neck. 'Did anyone hurt you?' he asked.

She looked at him with her big blue eyes and wet lashes, but it was obvious she didn't know what he was asking.

'How does she communicate with her parents?' Alice-Miranda asked. 'Does she understand sign language?'

'I think Laura's been teaching her,' Larry said.

Barnaby carried Matilda down to the house, where everyone was waiting in the kitchen. Hugh had called Darley's Plains. Laura was on her way with her parents, and to say she was excited was an understatement. She'd radioed Cam and Ted and they were en route too, but it would be a while before everyone arrived, given the vast distances they needed to cover.

Matilda spotted the room full of strangers and clung to Barnaby's neck until Lucas began to play peek-a-boo with her. She started to giggle.

Barnaby took the opportunity to put the child down on the table and check for any obvious injuries. Apart from some scratches – probably the result of tramping through the scrub – she looked to be fine, which made the man feel a lot better. She was covered in dirt, but a bath could wait until her mother arrived.

'Who's up for some hot chocolate?' Lawrence asked. He was keen to do something useful.

Lucas stunned everyone by signing the question to Matilda.

The girl's face brightened and she nodded.

'When did you learn how to sign?' Alice-Miranda asked.

Lucas grinned. 'I've been taking a class at school the past year – it's voluntary just at lunch-times once a week. I thought it was a good idea.'

'You never told me about that,' Lawrence said, impressed with his son.

'I guess I just forgot – there's so much going on,' Lucas shrugged.

Jacinta looked at the boy adoringly, wondering if there was anything Lucas couldn't do.

'That's brilliant, Lucas. Could you ask Matilda if anyone hurt her while she was lost?' Barnaby said.

The others looked at him. 'Why?' Jacinta asked.

'I just need to know,' Barnaby said.

Lucas looked at the girl and signed the question. She shook her head.

'Ask her if she saw anyone out there? Did anyone look after her?' Alice-Miranda said.

Matilda watched Lucas's hands, then nodded.

'You were right, Alice-Miranda. Someone must have found Matilda and brought her here to the homestead,' Hayden said.

'But for some reason they didn't want anyone to know – though they weren't very good at covering their tracks,' Alice-Miranda said. Matilda held her arms out towards the girl, who moved the child onto the chair between herself and Millie.

'Maybe they were travelling through,' Millie said.

'Or they're a fugitive on the run from the law,' Jacinta said dramatically.

No one wanted to think that was true, but nothing was outside the realms of possibility.

Larry stirred her mug of hot chocolate and lifted it to her lips. 'Mum says that there are lots of people who come to the outback to escape from something.'

For now, at least, whoever had brought Matilda to Hope Springs was a mystery.

'Wasn't Blue Dog supposed to be with her?' Hayden said.

'Yes,' Barnaby replied, 'but there's no sign of her anywhere. Could you ask Matilda about the dog, Lucas?'

The boy signed a question and Matilda turned her palms upwards and shrugged. 'I don't think she knows where Blue Dog is.'

Lawrence finished passing out the mugs of hot chocolate and found some biscuits. Matilda drank and ate everything she was offered, but soon started to fall asleep again. She crawled into Alice-Miranda's lap and nestled down, clearly very comfortable with her new friend.

'Come on, little one,' Barnaby said. He turned to Larry. 'I'm going to put her in with you girls.'

He picked up Matilda and carried her to the sleep-out. The boys, Jacinta and Millie all went back to bed, but Larry and Alice-Miranda were wide awake. They headed into the lounge room and sprawled out on the couches. Junie and Rusty joined them, Junie leaping into Alice-Miranda's lap and nuzzling her hand for attention.

'Do you think we'll ever find out who brought Matilda back?' Alice-Miranda asked.

Larry frowned. 'It's a strange one, that's for sure. They obviously don't want to be found, but maybe we can put our heads together and solve the mystery? If I didn't plan on taking over the station then I think I'd like to become a detective or, even better, a spy.'

'That sounds like fun,' Alice-Miranda said. 'Millie, Jacinta and I have been known to solve a few cases.'

'Tell me more,' Larry said. 'You mentioned something about a man who woke up from a coma yesterday. What's that story?'

'Oh yes, poor Mr and Mrs Parker,' Alice-Miranda began. 'It was terrible at the time . . .'

Larry was mesmerised and when Alice-Miranda came to the end of her tale, Larry told her about the time her family had gone on holidays to Kakadu and ended up surrounded by crocodiles on a river crossing. Alice-Miranda was on the edge of her seat. Over an hour passed, and it was only the sound of a diesel engine coming up the driveway that distracted the girls from their storytelling.

'Laura's here!' Larry yelled, and she and Alice-Miranda raced for the door as the rest of the family hauled themselves back out of bed.

Chapter 19

Sprocket was rudely awoken by a sudden blinding light and the loud noise of someone thumping the side of the ute. He looked up from where he lay, curled around tools and wedged between the edge of the tray and the old dog cage.

'Rise and shine, my friend.' The man who had kidnapped him from Dan's place thumped the vehicle again, sneering down at him.

Sprocket shielded his eyes from the rising sun. His nose was throbbing, and he could still taste blood in his mouth. Every bone in his body was aching too. He had no idea how long he'd been out. The last thing he remembered was deciding not to do a runner.

The brute handed him a water bottle. Sprocket hauled himself up against the back of the rear windscreen and unscrewed the lid. He sniffed first, wanting to make sure that the guy wasn't about to poison him, then gulped it down.

'Thanks,' he mumbled. 'Although I think calling me *your* friend is a stretch. None of *my* friends have ever punched me in the face.'

'I was just being polite like my mother taught me,' the man replied. He pulled a sandwich out of the esky in the cabin and passed half to Sprocket, who eyed it warily.

'Go on, take it,' the man said, waving the food under Sprocket's nose. 'I don't need you to die of starvation, you silly old coot.'

Sprocket took a good look at the fellow and understood why his nose hurt so much. The chap's arms rippled with muscles and his neck was the girth of a small tree trunk. What hair he had was shorn close to his head and there was a deep scar above his left eyebrow. His was a face you didn't forget, so Sprocket was pretty sure he'd never seen him before.

'Do you have a name?' Sprocket asked.

'That's on a need to know basis, and you don't need to know,' the bloke replied.

Sprocket ate the ham and cheese sandwich, which was far more delicious than he'd expected. Though maybe that was just because he hadn't had anything to eat since lunch the day before.

'Where are we?' Sprocket asked, standing up in the back of the tray. He turned three hundred and sixty degrees, but there wasn't a single landmark he knew. All he could see was miles and miles of red dirt plains and scrubby mulga trees with the odd rocky outcrop.

'That's not really your concern now, is it?' the man said.

'Well, it is, because I need you to point me in the right direction so I can be heading home.' Sprocket licked his finger and tried to wipe some of the crusty blood from his top lip. He wasn't terribly successful, merely smearing a red stain across his face.

The bloke walked back to the front of the truck and pulled out a piece of paper.

'You know what this is?' he asked, waving it at Sprocket, who shook his head. 'I think you do, you lying hound.'

'I have no idea what you're talking about!' Sprocket exclaimed.

'Yeah right. What were you doin' in that dugout then? I know it's not yours,' the man said, the friendly demeanour in his voice giving way to something harder.

'That dugout belongs to *my friend*, Taipan Dan. He's been away for a while and I wasn't sure if he was back, so I went to take a look,' Sprocket said.

'And you just let yourself in?' the other bloke said.

'Yes, because we're mates,' Sprocket said. 'What were you doing there?'

'I'm taking what's mine,' the man said. 'Dan thought he could hide it but nothin' gets past my missus. She realised the old man had what I need to get my dues – pity it wasn't before I'd driven halfway out here, but never mind. You were just unlucky to be there.'

'You're nothing but a common thief,' Sprocket said, shaking his head.

'And you're about to turn your hand to that skill too,' the man replied.

Sprocket frowned. 'What do you mean?'

'We're off to Hope Springs. I saw that damn kid grab the map that blew out the window and you're going to get it back for me,' the fellow threatened.

Sprocket looked at him as if he was mad. 'Why would I do that?' he said.

'Because if you don't, there's a ditch back there that wouldn't take long to turn into a grave,' the man snarled. 'And if you think about double crossing me – remember, I know where you live. Coober Pedy's a dangerous place for an old fella. Always a shame when they fall down a hole and never come out again.'

A lump rose in Sprocket's throat. 'Okay,' he squeaked. 'Will you let me go once I've found what you're after?'

'I'll think about it,' the man replied.

Chapter 20

It was almost midday by the time the Darley family took Matilda home. Cam had arrived a couple of hours after his wife with Ted, his brother-in-law, who was also the local sergeant from Coober Pedy.

Alice-Miranda had given the man her full statement and remembered to tell him about the white ute she'd seen yesterday afternoon. Unfortunately, the tracks from the vehicle near the shed weren't a lot to go on, though Ted did take away the blanket Matilda had lain on to see whether he could wangle some forensic testing down in the city. Because no crime had been committed, though, and Matilda was safe and unharmed, he didn't expect his superiors would want to spend resources on the investigation when there were more pressing matters at hand. He'd left before the others to settle a dispute between several claim holders at the pub in Coober Pedy.

After they'd waved the Darleys off, the family and friends trundled inside. 'I think a movie afternoon might be in order for you lot,' Barnaby said as he noticed all of the children yawning contagiously.

'The early start must be catching up,' Alice-Miranda said. 'But if there are jobs to do we'd much rather help.'

Millie frowned and yawned again. 'Not me. I'm exhausted.'

'Yeah, speak for yourself, Alice-Miranda. I need a nap,' Jacinta leaned her head on Lucas's shoulder.

'What about if we organise some lunch then, and you kids can choose something to watch,' Hugh said.

'What are you going to do, Daddy?' Alice-Miranda asked.

'I think we're heading out to make a start on that bore,' he said, looking at Barnaby, who nodded.

'Having seen the place from the air yesterday, we're going to have to check more than one of them,' Barnaby said.

'What do you mean, Dad?' Larry asked.

'The place is dry all over – not just the home paddocks,' the man replied as the phone rang.

Hayden ran to pick it up. 'Hi Mum,' he said. 'Laura and Ted have just taken Matilda home.'

There was a lull as Evie spoke on the other end of the line. A few minutes later, Hayden put his sister on. Larry didn't talk for long before she handed the phone to her father, while the others set about getting lunch ready and Jacinta and Lucas headed into the lounge room to browse through the collection of DVDs in the television cabinet.

'Mum said hello to everyone,' Larry announced, walking to the pantry and pulling out jars of Vegemite, peanut butter and jam.

'How is she?' Alice-Miranda asked.

'She's good,' Larry reported. 'Pretty relieved about Matilda. And Granny moved into the nursing home yesterday. There's a male nurse who's very funny and Granny has taken a shine to him, so it wasn't as difficult as Mum expected. But she still has lots of clearing out to do and probably won't be back for another couple of weeks.' Larry's sparkling eyes seemed to lose their twinkle. Alice-Miranda couldn't help noticing the sad look on Barnaby's face too.

She walked over to the man and asked quietly. 'Are you all right, Uncle Barnaby?'

The question caught him off guard and he brightened immediately, putting on a brave face.

'Yes, of course,' he said. 'I miss Evie, that's all. These distances never get any easier but, when you run a property, that's just how it is.'

Alice-Miranda leaned in and gave the man a hug around the middle.

'What's that for?' He looked at her, the crinkles in the corners of his eyes creasing into a smile.

'Just because,' the child said.

He kissed the top of her chocolate curls.

'Thank you, sweetheart,' he said.

'Dad's such a wuss,' Larry winked at Alice-Miranda. 'But we still love him anyway.' She nudged her father's arm as he walked past and he gave her a special grin.

'Lunch is ready!' Hugh called. Lucas and Jacinta stampeded in.

'What is it about the air out here that makes me feel hungry all the time?' Millie asked as she grabbed two slices of bread and spread them with butter.

'At least we haven't come across any more dinosaurs,' Jacinta said.

The others giggled.

'What?' Jacinta pulled a face. 'Stop making fun of me. It's true!'

Lucas nodded. 'I believe you, even if the others don't.'

'Please,' Millie rolled her eyes. 'Just because she's your girlfriend.'

Jacinta poked her tongue out at Millie. Alice-Miranda decided it was time to change the subject.

'So, what do you think is wrong with the bore, Uncle Barnaby?' she asked.

'I'm not sure, but I've got parts for just about any problem – though I might not have enough if more than one bore needs fixing. Seems odd to have multiple break downs at the same time. What I do know is that if I don't get it sorted, those three-minute showers are about to become a wash in a bucket – with shared water.'

'Three!' Jacinta frowned. 'Millie told me it was two.'

The red-haired girl chuckled. 'Do you know how much fun it's been hearing you complain about washing your hair in less time than it usually takes you to get wet?'

'Mean!' Jacinta fumed. 'I didn't have long enough to wash the conditioner out. No wonder I look all greasy.'

Fortunately the exchange was in relatively good humour. Jacinta had come a long way since her days as Winchesterfield-Downsfordvale's second-best tantrum thrower, although Alice-Miranda whispered to Millie that she should probably stop pushing her luck. Poor Jacinta had been a little fragile the past few days, especially since the incident with the frill-necked lizard.

Lunch was rounded out with cups of tea and cake before the three men stood up.

'Are you sure you don't need some help?' Alice-Miranda asked, but Barnaby and her father were adamant that they'd be fine. With any luck, they'd get on top of the water issue today and be able to start the mustering tomorrow. They'd need the children rested and all hands on deck for that.

*

Jacinta held up the three DVDs she and Lucas had narrowed the afternoon's viewing down to, so everyone could vote.

'Oh, we're not watching that again.' Millie grinned and shook her head when she realised that one they'd selected was *The Life and Times of Nellie Williams.* 'Besides, we've heard from a few people around here that it's total rubbish.'

'Jacinta's choice,' Lucas said with a chuckle.

'You said you wouldn't mind seeing it again,' Jacinta said, her jaw flapping open.

'Okay, I lied,' the boy confessed.

'We've watched it like a thousand times,' Larry said. 'Mum loves it – she'll be so disappointed that she missed out on meeting your dad. Don't tell him, but he's her movie star crush.'

Hayden raised his eyebrows. 'It's true. Dad's always teasing her about it.'

'He has that effect on lots of people,' Millie said, fanning herself with her hand. 'Mr Lipp, the old drama teacher at Fayle, was completely besotted with Lawrence until he fell in love with Frau Furtwangler.'

The children debated the merits of the other two movies on offer. One was a spy drama about twins whose lives were forever changed when they found out that their grandmother was in charge of the world's most important spy organisation, while the other was about a group of friends at boarding school. In the end they picked the spies. It seemed fitting, given there were a few mysteries in their midst at the moment.

'Who's up for popcorn?' Hayden asked.

There was a chorus of yeses. The boy headed back to the kitchen with Alice-Miranda in tow, while Larry showed Lucas how to put the movie on and Millie and Jacinta bagsed the best seats.

Hayden walked into the pantry, which was like a small supermarket with shelves neatly arranged and enough supplies to last for months. It also had a small built-in desk with a tall stool near the old phone on the wall.

'There,' Alice-Miranda pointed up high at some boxes.

Hayden climbed up the stepladder and threw three packets down. Alice-Miranda quickly read the instructions and put them one after the other into the microwave in the kitchen.

'I've been thinking about the bores. Could there be something in the water that's making them seize up?' Alice-Miranda asked. 'Like rust?'

Hayden shrugged. 'That's a big problem with bore water. It's high in iron, so it tastes terrible. We only use it for the shower and the toilets. That's why we have all those orange stains on the tiles and in the cistern. Mum says it's just about impossible to get rid of them, though she still tries.'

'I guess water is more precious than gold out here,' Alice-Miranda said. 'Or opals.'

'Sure is.' Hayden found three large bowls, and it wasn't long before they marched into the lounge room and took up their positions to watch the movie. Junie and Rusty had joined the group and were curled up together on the floor, Rusty's paw resting on the ginger cat's shoulder.

'You know, even if we do find that Taipan Dan guy, I don't think we can give Junie back,' Larry said. 'Rusty is in love, and he might not recover if he lost his new best friend.'

'I tend to agree,' Millie said. 'I've never seen a dog and cat adore each other like those two.'

'They're the cutest,' Jacinta agreed, then nudged Lucas.

He whispered, 'You're the cutest,' into her ear and she blushed.

Junie meowed loudly as if to agree and the children giggled.

They started the movie and before long the group was heavily invested, leaning forward in their seats and yelling at the screen. 'It's a treasure map!' Millie shouted. 'You need to match it up with a real map – a topographical one like we studied in geography last term.'

'That Max kid's probably already committed the entire world atlas to memory – he's pretty awesome,' Larry said.

The children clenched their fists, hearts racing.

'It's there!' Hayden pointed at the television.

That's it, Kensy! Come on. We need to find the jewels before anyone else does.' The boy on the screen shouted.

'This movie's fantastic,' Millie said as the music amped up and on the screen the twins hot-wired a motor scooter and started speeding through the streets of Berlin.

'I love all the puzzles, and how they have to work everything out,' Larry said.

Alice-Miranda was watching intently, but her mind had started to wander. She jumped up just as a car sped across the characters' paths.

'Where are you going?' Millie asked. 'Do you want us to pause it?'

But Alice-Miranda was already gone.

She raced to the sleep-out and rummaged around in her bag to find the jeans she'd been wearing the day they'd driven to Hope Springs. She pulled them out and checked the pocket to find the paper with the squiggly lines and the 'X'.

'Alice-Miranda!' Millie called as her feet thundered down the hallway. 'Are you coming back?'

'Sorry. That scene in the movie made me think of the piece of paper I found on the road and I wanted to make sure that I still had it,' Alice-Miranda apologised.

'Are you going to watch the end?' Millie asked. 'It's really exciting.'

Alice-Miranda nodded and put the page into her pocket. She'd have a look through Barnaby's old books and ledgers once the movie was finished.

Millie looped her arm through Alice-Miranda's and the pair scurried back to the lounge.

Hayden pressed play, and the friends sat enthralled by the final twenty minutes, though Alice-Miranda was willing the film to hurry up and finish so she could have a look at the old records in the office. The finale had danger aplenty, but in the end the twins emerged unscathed, the bad guys dealt with and their grandmother as proud as punch – though she was still a little disparaging about a few things they'd done.

'Wow, that woman is harsh,' Millie said. 'If I was as brave and clever as Kensy I'd tell her to back off, babe.'

'Max is so hot!' Jacinta remarked.

'Oh really?' Lucas smirked.

'Look out, Lucas,' Millie grinned.

'Haha,' Jacinta leaned her head against Lucas's shoulder.

'How long have you two been, you know, boyfriend and girlfriend?' Hayden asked. He'd never thought about the idea of a girlfriend – in fact, he hardly knew any girls other than Larry and Stormy. Yet he had found himself thinking a couple of times that Alice-Miranda was cute.

Jacinta looked at Lucas, a coy smile on her face.

'I can tell you,' Millie interjected. 'It's like this. Jacinta has had a massive crush on Lucas like forever – well, since Lucas came to Fayle School for Boys, actually maybe before that at Alice-Miranda's Aunt Charlotte's birthday party – and I think Lucas was always keen on her too, though they were utterly useless at sharing their feelings for quite some time and Jacinta would always deny it – even when her face would go red anytime he looked at her. So it's been going on for ages, but they had their first proper kiss when we were on a leadership camp in Scotland . . .'

'What!' Jacinta's eyes were huge. 'No one saw that!'

'Are you kidding? Why do you think Mr Ferguson never sent that photo from the park in Inverness to Aunty Gee? I heard him telling Miss Cranna that it was just as well he noticed you two kissing before he distributed the picture far and wide,' Millie said, to much giggling from the others.

'Anyway, then Jacinta went all crazy because she thought that Lucas was going to live with his mother in LA for a while next year and they had a bust up again, but they've vowed not to get too kissy-kissy yet because they'll get into trouble at school if they do.'

Larry snorted with laughter. Hayden and Alice-Miranda were giggling too.

'Well, I know who I'm going to employ to write my autobiography when I'm old and famous,' Lucas said. 'I had no idea you were so observant, Millie.'

'You mean such a busy body,' Jacinta said. 'I think she could give Mrs Parker a run for her money.'

Millie looked wounded. Her bottom lip trembled and her eyes filled with tears.

'Uh oh.' Alice-Miranda was about to intervene when Jacinta jumped up and walked over to the girl.

'Oh, for goodness sake, Millie, I didn't mean it.'

Millie's eye's crinkled and a grin came to her lips. 'Me either. I'm just an awesome actress, don't you think!'

'Oh, you monster!' Jacinta leapt on Millie and began tickling the girl's ribs.

'Larry!' Millie called. 'I need some help here.'

Within seconds, Larry had joined in and was attacking Jacinta, who squealed like a piglet. It was Lucas who came to her aid.

'Tickle monster!' Alice-Miranda shouted as she launched herself at Hayden. The six friends were giggling and wheezing and begging for mercy a few minutes later.

Millie rolled over and lay on her back. 'I haven't laughed that much in ages.'

'My sides hurt,' Larry got to her knees and smiled. It felt good to laugh.

'Next movie?' Millie panted as she crawled back up onto the lounge chair and caught her breath.

'Maybe later,' Larry said. 'I should try and get some water onto Mum's vegie patch. I'm going to steal some from Molly and Ralph's tanks, seeing that they're not here. I'll just have to find a hose long enough.'

'We can help,' Lucas said, glad to get out for some fresh air. Millie nodded. Jacinta wasn't quite so keen to leave the safety of the house, but she'd go if Lucas did.

'Do you mind if I stay in and have a poke about in the old ledgers in your father's study?' Alice-Miranda asked.

'Sure. Dad said you could,' Hayden replied. 'I'll help if you like. Wouldn't it be amazing to find the other half of that treasure map?'

Alice-Miranda smiled. 'That would be incredible. And yes please, I'd love a hand. Thanks.'

'Just make sure you find it,' Larry said, getting to her feet. 'We need a family holiday.'

And with that the children dispersed, leaving Junie and Rusty in peace.

Chapter 21

Barnaby Lewis's study was a large room at the front of the house, across the hall from the master bedroom. Floor-to-ceiling bookshelves of century-old cedar lined two walls, with a library ladder on a rail used to reach the highest points. An acreage of antique desk sat in the middle of the space, accompanied by a swivel chair that looked original. It was an imposing room, with portraits of Lewises past hanging from picture rails on the other two walls. They were mostly stern men with deeply-lined faces and skin like leather – no doubt the result of years of working outdoors in one of the harshest environments on earth.

There was a single photo of the station's female residents. The lady of the house stood in the centre of the frame, dressed in a fine long gown and a hat that could have been used as a shade umbrella; two young girls standing either side. They were surrounded by the household – Indigenous women and girls. Their dresses, simple long pinafores and, in keeping with the style of the times, there wasn't a smile among them – although Alice-Miranda thought one of the young women looked as if she was about to grin. It was a picture of a time long past. She couldn't help wondering about the staff – were they treated well and fairly? The way Hayden and Larry talked about Molly – she seemed more like a grandmother than an employee, and they seemed very close to Stormy and River too. Alice-Miranda hoped they'd be home soon so she could meet them all.

'Family photos,' Hayden commented, pointing to a picture on the other wall. 'That's my grandpa, Evan, and his brother, Chester. I'm not sure what happened to him. Molly just shakes her head when

I ask and Dad says he knows as much as we do. There is one story – see his finger?' Alice-Miranda peered in at the picture. The shot had been taken outside, the boys leaning over a post-and-rail fence. 'Chester's got a claw instead of a nail. Dad said he got it mangled in a motorbike chain and it grew back looking like a parrot's beak.'

'Oh, that's nasty,' the girl replied. She pointed at a portrait of a young man and woman in a silver frame on the desk. 'Who's that?'

'That's Grandpa again, and Grandma Thea. She was from Norway – can you imagine what a shock it would have been to come and live out here with all this heat and dust after the snowy landscape of Scandinavia? Dad doesn't talk about them much, but Molly says Grandma left Grandpa when Dad was only five. She went back to Norway and no one ever heard from her again. Pretty sad, don't you think? Molly said Grandpa died of a broken heart when he was forty-six.'

'That's tragic,' Alice-Miranda said. 'Families can be complicated, can't they?'

'Sure can,' Hayden said.

'Where should we begin?' Alice-Miranda asked, looking around the shelves.

Hayden pointed up to some slender green spines with gilt writing at the top of the bookcase. 'What about those? They look ancient.'

The boy climbed up and pulled down two books.

Alice-Miranda opened the first and scanned the contents of the yellowed pages. It was a ledger with farm accounts, and notes about feed and stock. There were also grocery lists and the names of people working on the station. The writing was similar to the script on the map page Alice-Miranda had found, but when she compared it closely, it definitely wasn't from the same author.

The second book contained almost identical information from a year later. The children continued their search but after investigating at least a dozen tomes, Hayden declared that they were probably looking in the wrong place.

'We need to find something with maps,' the boy declared.

'Hayden!' Larry called from the back door. 'Can you give us a hand out here?'

He looked at Alice-Miranda who gave him a nod. 'I'll put these away. You go,' she said.

'Are you sure?' Hayden said. He was quite

enjoying their task, and, never having had much of a look around the room himself, wondered at what treasures might be unearthed.

'Hayden!' Larry screeched.

'It sounds important,' Alice-Miranda said.

'See you in a bit,' the boy rolled his eyes. 'She's probably got the hose tangled up or something.' The boy gave a wave and scampered out of the room.

Alice-Miranda scaled the ladder to put the books back – several at a time. She was placing each one carefully onto the shelf when she spied something wedged at the back. It was a slim volume covered in a thick layer of dust.

'What's this?' she mumbled to herself, then stretched her arm and grabbed it.

Alice-Miranda scurried back down the ladder. The book was much smaller than the homestead's official ledgers. She opened the first page and began to read. It seemed to be a diary, but without dates. The owner was a mystery too, as there was no name in the front – or anywhere that she could see. She followed the scripted handwriting with her right pointer finger, some of the words more difficult to make out than others.

'C is causing trouble again. He needs to keep his thoughts in check and leave her alone. Nothing good will come of it. Father is incandescent, and if mother was still alive she wouldn't hear of it. C needs to spend some time in Adelaide and get the girl out of his system – there will be no mixed marriages in this family. Father will not allow it,' the girl read aloud.

Alice-Miranda hesitated. People should be allowed to marry whomever they want, but she knew history had dictated otherwise for such a long time. The girl wondered if she should put the book back where she found it, but there was something intriguing about the story. She didn't want to stop. It felt as if she was reading the most engrossing novel, except that in this case the people were real. She sat down on Barnaby's chair before continuing to read.

Everyone mentioned in the diary was referred to by a single initial, though a woman the writer had met received a more romantic description – her hair described as flaxen straw and her blue eyes like sapphires. The language was quite formal and old-fashioned but the handwriting seemed more modern than the ledgers. Most of the entries were about visitors and a terrible drought, but towards the middle, things took a darker turn.

'He's ruined everything. M brought the baby back to the station, and the minute Father laid eyes on the child, he insisted the boy be raised as one of us. What of my degree? All those years at medical school, wasted, and for what? C's illegitimate child. Not to mention the impact on my wife. It was hard enough T coming to live here after the promises I'd made of life in the city. Now she has a baby to look after – not even her own. I told Father the child should be raised by M – he's her nephew too, but the man won't hear of it. That boy will be the death of us all.

Alice-Miranda let out a tiny gasp. Hadn't Larry said yesterday that her grandfather was a doctor, but he never practised? He'd had to take over the station because something had happened to his older brother . . . Chester. *C's illegitimate child.* Could that be Chester? He must have fallen in love with one of the Indigenous women on the station – M's sister. Could that be Molly? Uncle Barnaby talked about Molly a lot, and treated her as family. Perhaps that's because she was. Something terrible must have happened for Chester and Molly's sister to abandon their baby.

'Father is dead. Doctors say it was a heart attack. There is no escaping this place now – I've gone over the books, and we're so heavily in debt that even if I sell, there won't be much left. T deserves better and, frankly, so does the boy. He is not without his charms – though I have found it hard to form any real bond.'

By the time Alice-Miranda arrived at the last page, her pulse was racing and tears welled in her eyes.

'T is gone and my heart has been shattered into a thousand tiny pieces. If only we'd have been able to have our own child – perhaps she would have stayed. This country is harsh, and she has been homesick for her own land so very different to here.'

Tears sprang to Alice-Miranda's eyes. From what Hayden had said about his grandparents, he had no idea about any of this. Alice-Miranda wondered if Uncle Barnaby knew – perhaps not. The girl had discovered more secrets than she knew what to do with – she only hoped that Molly would be back soon, because she had a feeling that the woman alone would know the right thing to do.

Alice-Miranda climbed up the ladder and tucked the diary back where she'd found it. Her head was swimming. For now, she wouldn't tell anyone what she'd learned. Some things were best left unsaid, and this was really none of her business.

Hayden poked his head around the door.

'Did you find anything?' he asked.

Alice-Miranda turned, her face brightening.

'No, I guess the page will remain a mystery for now,' the girl said, and jumped off the last rung of the ladder onto the ground. 'What was the emergency?'

'Goanna trying to break into the hen house,' Hayden said. 'But we shooed him away with a broom. Molly won't be happy if she comes back and is down a girl or two. She loves her chickens.'

'Was Jacinta there?' Alice-Miranda winced.

Hayden nodded. 'It's a wonder the big fella didn't run away after all the screaming, but we put her on Molly and Ralph's veranda, out of the way, and she finally calmed down.'

'I'd better come and see if she's okay,' Alice-Miranda said.

The pinging of two-stroke engines alerted the children to the return of Barnaby, Hugh and Lawrence.

Alice-Miranda was eager for a distraction and, to Hayden's surprise, grabbed the boy's hand and ran to the back door.

'Did you fix the bore?' the child asked.

'Didn't seem to be anything wrong with it,' Barnaby said. 'Except that we have no water pressure, despite the pump being in perfect working order. We're going to have to head further out and see if there are problems with the others.' He scrubbed at his face. 'But we need to get a mob in tomorrow too. Truck's coming to take them to market day after.'

'We can do the mustering,' Hayden said. 'Larry and me, and the other kids and Rusty.'

Barnaby looked at his son. 'You're sure you're up to it?'

'Yes please!' Alice-Miranda exclaimed. She couldn't wait to get on a horse and do something useful.

'Well, you'd just have to bring in a small herd from the western paddock. And I guess you and your sister have helped plenty of times before.' Barnaby gave the children a grin.

'We won't let you down, Dad,' Hayden said. Larry and the other kids had just arrived, Millie carrying a basket of eggs and Jacinta looking shell-shocked, for the umpteenth time this trip.

'What are we doing?' Larry asked.

'Dad's leaving us in charge of the mustering tomorrow,' Hayden said proudly.

'You mean he's put me in charge,' the girl said with a grin.

'Okay, Bossychops, whatever,' Hayden said, shaking his head. There was no point getting into an argument with Larry, and he had to admit he'd always been glad that she loved the farm more than he did – it meant there wasn't any pressure on him to continue the family legacy. That used to happen in the old days – the eldest boy always inherited the farm. And any other children stayed and worked, or left to set their own course in life. He wondered what had happened to his grand-father's brother. He'd been older than Grandpa Evan, so by rights the place should have been his. Barnaby hadn't had an answer when Hayden had asked him in the past, and Larry had told him to stop questioning it. According to her, the thought of growing up in the city was the worst thing ever.

'Come on then, let's get the kettle on,' Hugh said.

Alice-Miranda was staring across the yard towards Molly and Ralph's place as the others all traipsed up the back steps.

'Are you okay?' Hayden gave her a nudge.

Alice-Miranda flinched. 'Sure. Just thinking about something.' She turned and followed the rest of them inside.

Chapter 22

Alice-Miranda patted the horse's neck. 'Hello boy,' she cooed to the stringy chocolate gelding, who stood statue-still while she placed the bridle over his head. He opened his mouth and nibbled at the bit, but didn't object in the slightest. 'He's very placid. Not like my Bony – I'd have a chunk of hair missing by now.'

'Comatose, did you say?' Larry grinned and lifted the saddle onto her own bay steed, who shifted left and right until the girl growled at the beast. 'Zuki, cut it out, okay.' For a second the horse did as she was told, but kicked out as soon as Larry tried to do up the girth strap.

'I think Zuki and Bony would have quite a bit in common,' Alice-Miranda remarked.

Millie was standing further away with her grey mare, whose temperament seemed somewhere in between the other two. 'How come this horse is called Saki when yours is Zuki?' she asked. 'They're almost the same – don't you get them mixed up?'

'They have proper names,' Larry said. 'Your girl is Kawasaki and mine is Suzuki.'

Alice-Miranda chuckled. 'So you named the horses after brands of motorbikes?'

'Ha, that's funny,' Millie said. 'Harley, Zuki and Saki. Are there any others?'

'We have another pony called Beemer, and we used to have Honda, but she died a couple of years ago. Beemer is Storm's. She's a feisty little brute, though she's an angel for Stormy,' Larry explained. 'Last time I tried to ride her she dumped me in the most massive pile of manure. Oh, and Dad has Kingy – he's the only one that escaped the motorbike moniker.'

Hayden, Jacinta and Lucas had opted for *steel* instead of *real* ponies. Hayden was taking one of the 250cc motorbikes, and Jacinta and Lucas each had their own four-wheeler.

The group assembled near the driveway, with Rusty wagging his tail beside them and Junie yowling from the veranda of the homestead, annoyed to have been left behind.

Barnaby, Hugh and Lawrence had left at dawn to check several more of the bores.

'Okay, does everyone have a water bottle?' Larry asked.

There were nods all round.

'Food?'

More nodding heads.

'Two-ways?'

There was a collective 'yes'.

'Oh, I forgot the sunscreen,' Millie grimaced. She'd already lathered her face that morning, but had left it on the bathroom sink.

Alice-Miranda dug into her saddle bag and pulled out a tube. 'It's okay. I picked it up for you.' She passed it across to Millie, who said thanks.

'Right, then,' Larry said. 'We need to bring the herd back here to the yards. Dad says there's only about five hundred of them. The bigger mustering job starts tomorrow when we bring the rest in for drenching and marking.'

'What's drenching? Is that why you need the water fixed?' Jacinta asked.

Hayden grinned. 'It means treating the cattle for worms and ticks and other parasites, and then we have to make sure that they're all ear-tagged and branded.'

'Oh.' Jacinta pursed her lips. She still wasn't sure what all that meant.

'What's happening to the ones we're rounding up now?' Millie asked.

'Market,' Hayden said. 'Truck should be out first thing in the morning.'

'Keep an eye out for the escapees, because when one makes a run for it they usually try to take some friends with them,' Larry continued. 'Dad said the herd was close to the groundwater tanks when he and Uncle Hugh were flying around the other day, so let's hope they still are. It'll make our job much easier.'

Alice-Miranda was impressed with Larry's business-like approach. It was clear the girl knew exactly what she was doing.

Hayden gave his sister the thumbs up and dropped the clutch, speeding up the track with Lucas and Jacinta on his tail. Alice-Miranda, Millie and Larry trotted along behind the vehicles, but once they were through the gate, Larry urged Zuki into a canter.

Alice-Miranda couldn't believe how much she'd missed riding. Harley might have seemed like he was asleep earlier, but he came to life now, springing after Zuki. She loved the loping feel of the beast beneath her. The gelding had an easy gait despite being at least a hand taller than Bony.

The girls rode for about half an hour before Millie shouted and pointed at a brown and white cow heading towards them. They could see the dust from the motorbikes further away and, as it cleared, the rest of the mob came into view. Hayden and the others must have located the herd beyond the tanks the riders had just passed.

'Breakaways!' Larry called. 'Yah!' Zuki was off after them.

Alice-Miranda and Harley gave chase too, which was just as well given another of the steers spun around and began to run in the opposite direction. Alice-Miranda gripped the saddle with her thighs, leaning left and right as they caught up to the errant beast.

'Yah!' she shouted, and chased the cow at full speed back to the main mob.

Millie had spotted another couple of escapees further away and was off after them. Mustering was a lot like barrel racing, but in some ways safer as the western saddles out here had more to hang onto. She wondered if she'd have been able to manage quite the same manoeuvres on her regular dressage tack.

Larry slowed Zuki down to a walk and lifted her Akubra, wiping the sweat from her brow. For the moment, the herd was behaving. She glanced over to Millie and Alice-Miranda, who were to her right, and gave the girls a nod. Millie pulled her water bottle from the saddle bag and took a swig.

The team herded the cattle back towards the homestead, the three girls bringing up the rear, with the cows flanked on each side by Hayden and Jacinta. Lucas made himself available to give chase where he was needed.

The children were having the time of their lives, and Alice-Miranda had all but forgotten about what she'd read the day before.

'Come on,' Larry threw her right hand forward. 'Let's bring them home.'

★

'How do you know there's nobody about?' Sprocket looked at the man beside him as they drove along the track to the west of the Hope Springs homestead.

'I told you. I watched them leave – I can see an ant on top of a fence post with those binoculars.'

'But what if they come back while we're inside?' Sprocket picked at his face. He wasn't keen to be caught trespassing on this villain's business.

'While *you're* inside. The three blokes set off at the crack of dawn, which tells me they've got a big day ahead of them, and when the kids left they took horses and bikes. Given it's mustering season, I'd say they're going to be away for quite some time too,' the man replied. 'Molly and Ralph and their crew are away on Sorry Business. Saw them come through last month – the kids confirmed it when they stopped at the roadhouse on their way here.'

Sprocket looked at him. 'How do you know who lives here?'

The man turned and glared. 'That's none of your concern.'

'Well, what am I supposed to do if I get caught?' Sprocket asked. He wasn't willing to let this go.

'Sit down and have a cup of tea and piece of cake,' the fellow said.

'Oh, good. That sounds nice. I could do with a cuppa, and country hospitality is always impressive,' Sprocket replied. The man clipped him over the top of the head.

'What?' Sprocket grimaced.

'You really are a grade A moron. You're not going to get caught, that's what you're going to do. I know where you live, McGinty, and those mine shafts are pretty unforgiving. If you tell a soul about our little arrangement here, then you had better say goodbye to anyone you've ever cared about,' the man threatened.

Sprocket swallowed hard. The man pulled the white ute around to the back of the smaller house, away from the homestead.

Sprocket opened the door and hopped out.

'Now find that piece of paper. The girl had it. The one with the curly brown hair,' the man replied.

Sprocket knew he meant Alice-Miranda, but where he'd find a half a page of paper in a homestead the size of the Lewis place was anyone's guess.

He looked left and right and over his shoulder before he scurried, on the balls of his feet, around the corner of the house to the main homestead. Pausing, he picked up a pebble and threw it on the roof, just in case someone had stayed behind. After waiting a few moments he was convinced there was no one home, and darted inside to find the place deserted . . .

. . . except for a fat ginger cat called Junie that he was extremely surprised to see.

Chapter 23

Barnaby Lewis looked at the bore. He couldn't work out what was wrong for the life of him. The pump was in perfect order and the pipes were good. There was just no water.

'Has the well run dry?' Lawrence asked.

'I hope not,' Barnaby said. 'The Great Artesian Basin supplies a huge amount of the outback groundwater for Australia. If that's shot then we've all had it. We've had problems with flow before — too many bores reducing the water pressure – but this doesn't add up. We've never had *no* water. It's going to cost a fortune if we have to sink another bore, and it'll take me at least a week to get things organised.'

'Barnaby,' Hugh said, separating a section of the pipe at the elbow join. 'What's this?'

The man peered at the contraption. He knew the workings of these things inside and out, and he'd never seen anything like it before. He pulled out the piece of metal and examined it closely.

'Is it a part that's come loose, perhaps?' Hugh asked. Lawrence was keeping quiet, as his knowledge of bores and pumps was non-existent. He was just happy to help with the carrying and lifting.

'No, it's just not meant to be there,' Barnaby said.

'My guess is that's created a blockage, then,' Hugh said, taking the device from his friend and placing it back where he'd found it. 'It fits inside here and creates a barrier.' Unlike Lawrence, Hugh had gained quite a deal of knowledge about bores and pumps from his time spent on the station. He'd even put it to use over the ensuing years, on various Kennington's farming projects.

'It makes no sense. I'm almost inclined to think it's been tampered with, but sabotage out here is unthinkable,' Barnaby said.

'Good heavens!' Lawrence exclaimed. 'Who'd want to do that?'

Barnaby shook his head. 'I have some ideas.' He was thinking about that run-in Cam had had with the new manager of Saxby Downs. The man had accused Cam of thieving water – maybe he'd just been trying to throw everyone off the scent of his own misdeeds.

'Let's put it back together without the additional part and see what happens,' Hugh suggested.

The men quickly set about doing just that, and half an hour later water was flowing freely again.

'So do you think it's a one-off?' Lawrence asked.

Barnaby shrugged. 'Impossible to say until we check the rest of them. We might as well keep going. If that extra part makes another appearance then I'll be calling Ted at the police station in Coober Pedy.'

Hugh nodded. 'How far to the next one?'

'About an hour's ride,' Barnaby said as he walked back to his bike and hopped on. He'd just kick-started the engine when there was a shriek from Lawrence.

'What's the matter?' Hugh called over the pinging of the bike. 'Shut it off!' he shouted to Barnaby, waving his arms about.

Lawrence's face was ashen as Hugh ran to him. Barnaby turned and caught sight of the brown snake slithering away towards the holding tank.

'Oh geez, mate,' Barnaby opened the metal toolbox that was strapped to the back of his bike and pulled out a crepe bandage. He wasn't taking any chances.

'I thought it was a stick caught up under the bike. I bent down and the little blighter got me. Is it bad?' Lawrence said.

He held out his arm, showing two puncture marks just above his left wrist.

Barnaby could only wish that the snake had been a 'little blighter'. He would have reckoned the thing was at least seven feet long, and healthy too.

'Okay, I need you to get off the bike and lie down. Stay as still as you can. You'll be fine, but it's really important that you keep calm and don't move,' Barnaby said as he wrapped the bandage firmly from the top of Lawrence's arm all the way down to his wrist to stop the spread of the venom.

Lawrence was already beginning to feel light-headed. Whether that was from the poison or the shock, he didn't know. But one thing was for sure, he wasn't planning to die of a snake bite in the middle of the Australian outback. Charlotte wouldn't be the least bit impressed – he'd promised her this wouldn't happen. In hindsight, he shouldn't have even mentioned the snakes. She hadn't liked the idea of them at all.

Barnaby grabbed the two-way radio and called the Royal Flying Doctor Service, but he didn't get the answer he hoped for. The closest plane had just left for the scene of a rollover hundreds of kilometres away.

'Okay, we've got some antivenene in the freezer back at the house,' he said.

'I thought the kids said you used it on the cat,' Hugh reminded the man. 'Unless you've got more.' He mentally crossed his fingers.

Barnaby nursed his forehead in his hand. 'Oh heck, you're right. I ordered another phial, but I haven't been to town to pick it up. Right, I'm going for the chopper,' Barnaby said. Flying Lawrence straight to the hospital at Coober Pedy was his best chance. It was impossible to know if he'd been envenomated but they couldn't take any risks.

'We're coming with you. Surely it's going to be better than waiting out here. Lawrence can pillion behind you. We can tie him on with some octopus straps if it comes to that,' Hugh suggested.

Barnaby nodded. Within a few minutes they were ready to leave.

The men sped along the bush tracks and through the paddocks as fast as they dared. Lawrence was clinging to Barnaby's back, although at one stage Barnaby thought the actor was losing his grip and slowed to make sure that he was still conscious.

'Come on, mate, stay with us,' Barnaby urged as Hugh hopped off his bike and checked on his brother-in-law. Lawrence was still awake, but visibly weaker with sweat streaming from his temples.

By the time they arrived at the hangar, Lawrence's breathing was shallow and he was having difficulty keeping his eyes open.

Barnaby raced in and prepped the aircraft, then pulled it out using the specially designed trolley.

Hugh had moved Lawrence onto the ground so he could rest more comfortably. Together, the men loaded him into the back seat of the chopper – it was fortunate they had a four-seater as Barnaby wouldn't have wanted to transport the injured man on his own.

'What about the kids?' Hugh shouted over the whine of the propellers as they slowly began to rotate.

'We'll call them once he's safe. They'll still be hours coming in with the cattle,' Barnaby said.

Hugh wasn't sure it's what he'd have done, and he didn't even want to think about the fact that where there was one snake there were bound to be more. Barnaby and Evie had lived out here for years without anyone being bitten though, so surely this was just a case of bad luck. Lawrence was going to be fine – he had to stay positive. In the future they'd all tell the tale of his miraculous recovery after being bitten by a huge western brown, but right now they just had to get him to hospital and make sure that he survived.

Sprocket McGinty had swallowed hard as he heard the ping of at least two motorbikes approaching the homestead. 'Oh geez, someone's back.' He'd looked around and wondered where he could hide, then peered through the louvred back windows into the empty yard.

He still hadn't found the map. His captor would be wondering what was taking so long, but there was no point returning empty-handed. He really didn't want to end up in the ditch back down the road. Sprocket began to hatch a plan. It would be much easier to get the document from Alice-Miranda herself. She knew who he was and he was a friend of her father's. Besides, the page wasn't hers to start with. He'd just ask her.

The motorbike engines had stopped a few minutes ago and Sprocket was still waiting, unhidden, for someone to return to the house. He'd just say that he had a lead on Dan and had dropped in to check whether they'd seen him. Except that Sprocket remembered he didn't have a car so they might question how he'd got there. He ran his tongue over the outside of his teeth and realised he was drier than a desert spring as the *shoosh shoosh shoosh* of a helicopter's rotors filled the air. Sprocket was surprised to see the blue R44 lift into the sky over the back of the sheds. It looked like there were three people on board. If that was the case, then maybe he was in the clear for a while yet.

He looked around the sleep-out. He'd made a terrible mess. Alice-Miranda's suitcase hadn't been hard to find, given it had a name tag, but perhaps upending the contents all over the floor hadn't been his smartest idea. Junie had followed him into the room and was now meowing her disapproval.

'It's not my fault, cat. You'd turn the place upside down too if you had that thug breathing down your neck. And what are you doing here anyway? Where's Dan?' he said to the cat, who meowed a reply to every question. Trouble was, Sprocket couldn't understand 'cat'.

He jumped from one leg to the other as if doing a Scottish jig. It was a nervous affliction, though sometimes he just liked to dance. He had no idea when the others would return. It could be any moment.

Sprocket's ears were still on high alert as he began to stuff the clothes back into the suitcase before remembering the child was neat. Everything in her suitcase had been folded and placed inside, not thrown haphazard like he was doing.

Sprocket was usually neat by nature too – it's just he was in a hurry. Though no one was likely to believe it, he'd actually attended a rather posh boarding school as a boy. He knew how to make beds with hospital corners and fold washing. Living out here however, his wardrobe was somewhat limited – underpants, a blue singlet and a pair of stubbies for each day of the week was all he needed and therefore didn't require much attention.

'Okay, Junie, you go and have a look and let me know if the coast is clear?' he said to the cat, who scampered out the door.

He'd go and explain his plan to the old bruiser, and drive the ute around to the back of the house so it looked like he'd brought his own vehicle. Then he'd wait for the kids to come home. He was sure he'd have that page by tonight, no matter what.

Chapter 24

It was just after four when Larry shut the gate on the herd and the children's work for the day was almost done. The cattle were now in the home paddock behind the sheds.

'Good job, everyone!' the girl called.

Hayden had already checked the water troughs and found them empty, so had gone to run a hose from one of the rainwater tanks at the back of Molly and Ralph's place. Obviously his father hadn't fixed the problem yet.

Alice-Miranda slid down from Harley's saddle and gave the horse's neck a rub. 'Thank you for looking after me out there. You're a lovely boy – much better behaved than my Bony.' Despite this, Alice-Miranda still missed her own naughty beast. Bony might have been tricky at times, but she had to admit his personality was larger than life.

Millie leapt off Saki and checked the mare's feet. She was worried that the horse had seemed a bit lame on the way in and soon saw the problem – a stone lodged in Saki's hoof.

Jacinta and Lucas had already returned their four wheelers to the shed and walked back to the yards to help Hayden.

'Should we give these guys a wash down and some dinner before we turn them out?' Alice-Miranda asked, garnering a nod from Larry.

'Unfortunately it will be more a bucket rinse than a proper shower,' the girl said. They walked the horses around to the stalls at the back of the machinery shed, where Millie quickly located a hoof pick and dealt with Saki's discomfort. The girls spent the next half hour tending to the horses before they were turned out into the home paddock up behind the hangar.

As they walked back down towards the house, they noticed two bikes in the shed in place of the helicopter.

'Did your dad say anything about taking the chopper out today?' Alice-Miranda asked Larry, who shook her head.

'Dad hates flying,' she said. 'He does it if he absolutely has to – like searching for Matilda – but otherwise he leaves all the mustering to Buddy. I think he had a close call a few years back, but he won't talk about it.'

'I wonder why there's only two bikes,' Millie said.

'Maybe the other one's in the machinery shed,' Alice-Miranda suggested. The girls took a peek when they went past, but it wasn't there.

'Maybe they had to head out further than Dad had originally planned,' Larry said.

The mystery was abandoned as they rounded the corner to see the white ute that had sat deserted on the side of the road the other day parked near the house, with Sprocket McGinty leaning on the bonnet.

'G'day, girls, how'd ya be?' Sprocket grinned, his teeth just about blinding the three of them with their glimmer.

Millie shielded her eyes. 'Close your mouth, Sprocket. You could permanently injure something with those fangs of yours.'

The man chuckled. Larry and Alice-Miranda did too.

Alice-Miranda noticed the blood encrusted around Sprocket's nose and on his chin. 'Are you hurt?' she asked urgently, pointing to his face.

Sprocket flinched, realising that he should have had a wash when he was in the house earlier. 'No, I just have a drippy snoz sometimes. Didn't realise it was bad,' he said.

'So this is *your* ute?' Alice-Miranda said. 'We saw it parked on the side of the road in the middle of nowhere the day we drove out – we were all a little worried as it seemed a strange place to leave a car – and with the door open too.'

'I don't usually leave the door open,' Sprocket mumbled to himself. 'Is Hugh with Two about?'

'Daddy and Uncle Barnaby and Uncle Lawrence are out checking the bores. There's a problem with the water,' the child explained. 'We're not sure when they'll be back. This is Larry, she's Uncle Barnaby's daughter.'

'Hello,' the girl nodded.

'That's a fine name you've got there,' Sprocket said. 'Same as mine actually. Just no one's used it in about fifty years.'

The girl broke into a grin. 'Thank you. I think it's an excellent name too. Would you like a cup of tea or a cool drink?'

'Is the Pope a Catholic?' the man replied as he followed the girls up the steps and into the house. 'Mind if I use your facilities? Don't fuss, I know where they are.'

Larry looked at him suspiciously. Sprocket recoiled. 'I mean, I have no idea where they are so you'll have to point me in the right direction, if you please?'

Larry frowned. 'Follow me,' she said, and led Sprocket down the hallway. 'Just in there.'

She sprinted back to the kitchen. 'Is that the crazy guy you went to visit before you came out here? The one who was doing an extension with dynamite?'

'One and the same,' Millie said. 'He's bonkers.'

'He might be slightly eccentric, but I think Mr Sprocket has a heart of gold. He saved Daddy's backside – quite literally.'

The girls giggled at Alice-Miranda's joke. There had been a discussion about Sprocket's lifesaving rescue during dinner the other night.

'I wonder what he's doing here?' Millie said.

They didn't have to wait long to find out.

Alice-Miranda had just retrieved six cups for the children's drinks and flicked the switch on the kettle when the man returned, his hair dripping wet.

Larry looked at him and frowned. 'Did you have a shower?'

'I limited myself to a minute. Barely got wet, but I've felt like a grub ever since . . . well never mind,' the man said. 'Found a towel on the shelf. Hope you don't mind – I know country folks are renowned for their hospitality.'

Millie looked at Larry, who kept a straight face and managed not to betray what she was really thinking. Certainly, her parents were generous hosts, though her mother would have been mortified – Evie always directed the stockmen and other workers to one of the cottages, as the house was her sanctuary and strictly reserved for family and invited guests.

'So, what are you doing out here?' Alice-Miranda asked as she finished making the man's tea and sat it down in front of him.

He picked up a teaspoon and the girls watched, mesmerised, as he heaped eight giant scoops of sugar into the cup.

'Aren't you going to stir that?' Millie asked.

Sprocket pulled a face. 'Good grief, no. I don't like it sweet.'

The girls chuckled as he lifted the cup to his lips.

'I thought I had a lead on Taipan Dan, but it's proven a dead end. Anyway, given I was so close to Hope Springs I thought I'd come and see how you were all faring,' the man said. 'And blow me down if you don't have Junie here with you. So maybe my lead isn't as dead as I thought.'

None of that was true, of course, though he *had* been shocked to see the cat.

'We found her on the road about half an hour before we saw your car,' Alice-Miranda said.

'My car? Where did you see my car?' he asked. 'Haven't seen it myself for a while actually.'

'Your white ute,' Alice-Miranda said, confused. 'The one that's sitting outside the back of the house at the moment.'

'Oh, that car, yes of course,' Sprocket frowned and lifted the cup to his lips. 'Lovely brew. My compliments to the tea lady.'

'So where were you when we found the ute?' Alice-Miranda asked.

'We called to see if there was anyone about. You mustn't have heard us,' Millie said.

'I was um, ah, indisposed,' the man replied. 'Had to walk a mile to find some privacy and then hope I didn't get bitten on the bum by a brown.'

The girls giggled. 'Absolutely understandable,' Alice-Miranda said.

Jacinta, Lucas and Hayden barrelled through the back door and were surprised to see the man sitting in the kitchen and holding court at the end of the table.

'Mr Sprocket, you remember Jacinta and Lucas and this is our friend Hayden, Larry's older brother,' Alice-Miranda took care of the introductions.

The children all said their hellos and grabbed some drinks.

'We've been out mustering,' Hayden said. 'It's thirsty work.'

The man nodded.

'Has anyone heard from Dad?' the boy asked.

The children shook their heads. 'He's taken the chopper. We could try him on the radio,' Larry suggested. The girl stood up and walked into the pantry, where she picked up the handset. There was a crackle of static over the airwaves. She held the microphone in front of her mouth and pressed the button on the side.

'This is Hope Springs to Victor Hotel Hotel Sierra Tango, come in please,' Larry said.

But there was no response. She tried again with the same result.

Alice-Miranda had hopped up to join the girl. 'What if I just call Daddy's mobile?'

'You probably won't get him. The coverage out here is patchy at best,' Larry said.

Alice-Miranda decided to try anyway. She picked up the ancient phone on the wall and dialled the number.

'Hello Daddy,' she said, and gave Larry a thumbs up. 'Where are you?'

'Oh my goodness, that's terrible,' the child gasped. Larry looked at her anxiously. 'Will he be all right?'

Larry was leaping about asking her who she was talking about, but clearly Alice-Miranda was still receiving information.

'Does Aunt Charlotte know?' Alice-Miranda asked.

Larry almost felt guilty for breathing a sigh of relief – it wasn't her father or mother who were in trouble – though she was still desperate to find out what was going on.

'We'll be fine, Daddy. Actually Mr Sprocket is here. He was in the neighbourhood and dropped in. Would you like me to ask if he can stay until you and Uncle Barnaby return? I know we'd be fine on our own. I just suspect the adults will feel more comfortable if there is another adult about – even though, to tell you the truth, Daddy,' she lowered her voice to a whisper and partially covered the handset, 'I think Mr Sprocket might be in more need of looking after than we are.' Her voice went back to its usual volume. 'Tell Uncle Barnaby that we got the cattle in.'

There was a pause again. Her father was speaking. 'Really? Sabotage? That's awful. Does Uncle Barnaby have any idea who might be responsible?'

There was another lull. 'Don't worry – we'll keep an eye out for anything unusual. It's probably a good thing Mr Sprocket's here now then.

Give Uncle Lawrence our love. Goodbye, Daddy,' the girl said, and promptly hung up.

'What's happened?' Larry demanded.

'I'd best tell everyone,' Alice-Miranda said, and walked out into the kitchen with Larry right behind her.

'So where are they?' Lucas asked.

'At the hospital in Coober Pedy. Uncle Lawrence was bitten by a snake, but they say he's going to make a full recovery. Daddy and Uncle Barnaby are staying with him for now though, until he's feeling properly better,' the girl explained.

Jacinta's mouth gaped open and Lucas's face turned pale.

'Daddy says you mustn't worry. Uncle Lawrence is fine. He's had a dose of antivenene and is awake and talking,' Alice-Miranda said. 'It's getting too late for Uncle Barnaby and Daddy to fly back and they don't have another vehicle in town, so they'll have to stay overnight and see how Uncle Lawrence is in the morning.'

'I've got one,' Sprocket said. 'A vehicle that is. If they can get themselves up to the hideaway they're welcome to it. Come to think of it, it might not start and I can't actually remember where the keys are and, oh no, they can't. It's parked out the back here isn't it?'

The children gave each other quizzical looks. The man seemed very confused about his car.

Sprocket took a slurp of tea. 'What got him? Inland taipan or a western brown?'

'Daddy said they think it was a brown snake but either way he's terribly lucky,' Alice-Miranda said.

But Jacinta wasn't feeling that way at all. Fat tears spilled onto the top of her cheeks and she started to cry. 'Why did that have to happen? I hate the outback!'

Lucas put his arm around her and she turned and sobbed into his chest. The boy was feeling wobbly at his father's close call himself, so he was glad to have someone to hold onto.

Alice-Miranda could understand that it was a big shock.

'There, there, Jacinta,' Sprocket gave her a grin. 'The outback is magnificent – and honestly, apart from all the things that are trying to kill you, it really is one of the safest places on earth. I bet this homestead's never been locked up once since it was built. The family probably doesn't even own a set of keys.' He thought about the irony of his words,

236

given his captor was now holed up in one of the staff dongas waiting for him to return with a map he was about to steal from a child.

'That's true,' Hayden said. 'We never lock anything, and the keys are always in the cars and the motorbikes. You never know when you might want to make a quick getaway.'

None of that was making Jacinta feel any better. She wished she had a pair of ruby slippers and could click her heels together and go home.

'Mr Sprocket, Daddy asked if you'd mind staying with us until he gets back.' Alice-Miranda said. 'He said he'd feel better knowing there was another adult here. Especially because Uncle Barnaby thinks that someone is tampering with the bores and stealing Hope Springs' water.'

'What!' Larry exploded. 'Just wait until I get my hands on whoever that low-life is. Did your father say who they think it could be?'

Alice-Miranda shook her head. Sprocket was staring off into the distance as if he was in another world.

Alice-Miranda prompted him again. 'Mr Sprocket, are you able to stay with us? I'd like to tell Daddy what's happening.'

Sprocket flinched and broke into a grin. It was fortunate there were no reflective surfaces in the kitchen. 'Yes, of course, it would be my honour,' he said. 'And I insist on cooking you all dinner. It will be a Sprocket special.'

The children looked at one another, wondering what that might be.

'Got me some roadkill in the back of the ute,' he winked. 'Bit of roo.'

Jacinta shuddered. 'I'm not eating that.' She jumped up and ran out of the room and down the hallway.

'I was kidding. I don't eat roadkill either. Well, not unless I'm *really* desperate and it's *really* fresh,' he said.

'Probably best not to make jokes like that at the moment, Sprocket,' Lucas said, and stood up to find Jacinta. 'She's feeling a little sensitive.'

'Sorry,' Sprocket replied, and sounded as if he meant it. 'You got any mince in the freezer? I do a mean spaghetti bolognaise. I'm not actually a bad cook and it'd be nice to make something for a crowd. Don't tend to cook for one very often and I don't fancy another tin of baked beans – I hate the darn things.'

Larry nodded and Alice-Miranda gave him a smile. 'Thank you, Mr Sprocket. That sounds delicious and we'd be very happy to help you.'

Sprocket needed to get out and tell Old Mate what he was up to, but at least he'd bought himself some more time. Besides he couldn't let Hugh with Two down – he'd promised to stay with the kids and that's exactly what he would do. And then perhaps he could also work out how he was going to get home in one piece.

Chapter 25

Alice-Miranda phoned her father back, then fielded calls from her mother and Evie too. She assured everyone that they were absolutely fine, although it didn't help that, during her conversation with Cecelia, Sprocket splashed boiling water on himself while draining the pasta and let out a string of swear words that would make a shearer blush.

Sprocket apologised profusely, admitting that there were only two things that brought pro-fanities to his lips – physical pain and ultimate stupidity – and he'd just given himself a double dose.

Dinner smelt delicious. The children helped set the table and Jacinta emerged from where she and Lucas had been watching another movie. The boy had suggested that it might be a welcome distraction for both of them and it seemed to have worked. Jacinta appeared to be in a much more positive frame of mind.

'Now would you like some too, Junie?' Sprocket asked the cat, who meowed loudly in reply. He heaped some pasta and bolognaise onto a plate and set it on the floor, only for Junie to stick her nose in the air and walk around it, flicking her tail.

'Sorry, love, I forgot,' he said. He picked the plate up and placed it on the table beside Larry. Junie leapt onto the chair and stood up with her paws on the table, waiting until everyone else was seated before she tucked in.

'That cat has better table manners than most people I know,' Sprocket said. 'Dan's taught her well.'

Millie giggled. 'Apart from the fact that my mother would be horrified to see an animal eating at the table with us, I tend to agree. It's almost like she's human.'

'You said you had a lead on Taipan Dan?' Alice-Miranda said. 'Do you know where he is?'

Sprocket shook his head. 'I don't know, but pounds to peanuts something untoward has happened to the silly old coot. There's no way he'd leave that cat of his stranded on the side of the road.'

'Perhaps we should call Sergeant Ted and tell him your suspicions,' Alice-Miranda suggested. 'If something has happened then shouldn't the police be searching for him?'

'No,' Sprocket said emphatically. 'No police.'

The children wondered why he was so adamant, but were all too exhausted to argue. Their day out mustering was catching up. A contagion of yawns swept the table.

Sprocket was thinking about how he could get Alice-Miranda to hand over the page his captor thought she had. He had a brainwave. It was the cleverest thought he'd had all day.

'When you found my ute out there on the road, you didn't happen to see a map, did you?' he asked, then sucked a long strand of spaghetti through his shiny teeth, making a horrible schlurping sound in the process.

'What sort of map?' Millie asked.

'Well, kind of like an old . . . um . . . a scrap of paper, about this big.' He held his hands about thirty centimetres apart, then brought them in a bit, then out again. Truthfully, he had no idea what he was looking for. The idiot who'd sent him to get it hadn't given him much to work with.

Alice-Miranda wriggled in her seat to pull something out of her back pocket. She'd had it with her the whole time. 'Do you mean this? I found it on the road so I wasn't sure where it had come from, but it makes perfect sense now. It must have blown out of your car.' She flattened it out on the table. 'It has the words "Hope Springs" in the bottom corner so I thought it must have had something to do with the station – that's why I took it with me. I am sorry.'

'You little ripper!' Sprocket could barely contain his glee.

'What is it?' Hayden asked.

'Um, ah, um.' The man had no answer for that – he didn't have a clue himself.

'We thought it might be part of a treasure map,' Alice-Miranda said. 'But half seems to be missing, so it wouldn't be much use. We thought the other half might be in the study.'

Sprocket tucked into his dinner and tried to ignore the girl's chatter, but she was a persistent character.

'That would be exciting – if it was a treasure map,' she said, to the agreement of the other kids.

'But if there was treasure here, wouldn't it belong to us,' Larry said.

Sprocket looked up and wiped a smear of tomato sauce from his lip with the paper napkin.

'It's not here,' he shook his head then realised that's exactly what it was – a treasure map. That's why the big fella had sent him to get it. 'See that,' he pointed at the words and managed to slop a big blob of red on the middle of it. 'Oops, I'm a klutz, aren't I. No wonder my mother left me under a bush to be raised by dingoes.'

Jacinta glared at the man. 'That's not true.' She paused. 'Is it?'

Lucas patted her arm. 'He's joking.'

'I wouldn't be so sure of that, young man. I can show you the marks where my dog-mother used to drag me around with her pups.' He pointed at his neck, which was peppered with strange scars.

'Ew!' Jacinta shuddered.

'Mr Sprocket is kidding, Jacinta. Please don't be upset. I know that he grew up in a very respectable family in Melbourne and went to boarding school just like us,' Alice-Miranda explained.

Sprocket looked at her, his blue bug eyes wide. 'How would you know that?'

'Daddy told me. He said that you went bush as a young man and loved it so much you gave up the city life. He said that there are lots of people in Coober Pedy with interesting stories like yours. Some people choose the bush and for others the bush chooses them.'

'That Hugh with Two always was a smart fella,' Sprocket said.

'Well, I don't choose the bush – ever,' Jacinta said.

'So is it a treasure map?' Larry asked again.

'I'm not really sure,' Sprocket lied. 'It's just something I've had for a long time – like a talisman that I keep close. I think it's going to bring me good luck,' he said.

He couldn't stop thinking about what Alice-Miranda had said about there being another half. If he could find that, then surely he could negotiate his release and the hairy brute would leave him alone. They could forget any of this happened, couldn't they?

Sprocket stood up from the table and stretched his arms above his head.

'Goodnight, kids,' he said.

Millie looked at the kitchen clock. 'Um, it's half past seven.'

'Is it that late? Goodness me. Way past my bedtime,' he said. 'I'll just be stretching out in the swag in the garden. See you in the morning.'

'Sprocket, Lawrence was bitten by a brown snake this afternoon. Do you really want to sleep in a swag outside on the ground?' Jacinta asked.

The man frowned. 'The movie star was deadset unlucky. I can tell you now that while this country is home to some of the deadliest snakes on earth, bite rates are low and no more than two people a year die. I agree that's two too many, but statistically you're in much greater danger of kicking the bucket from falling out of bed, which I won't do if I'm lying on the ground. Anyway, snakes don't like us much either and only really attack if we've got in their way – it's quite likely Lawrence stepped on the poor blighter, or something like that.'

None of that made Jacinta feel much better at all. She was just glad they weren't going camping on this trip.

'Sprocket, you can sleep in one of the staff dongas if you like,' Hayden offered. 'They're not locked. Just choose one.'

'Oh, that's very kind of you, young man. I'll have a think about that. Anyway, night all,' Sprocket said then walked to the door. He turned. 'I shouldn't leave you with the washing up though, should I?'

Alice-Miranda had already stood up to clear the plates. 'It's all right. You did the cooking. We can clean up.'

And with that, the man scampered down the hallway and out the back door.

Dan had no idea how long he'd been out. His mouth felt like the Simpson Desert and he could barely conjure enough saliva to lick his crusty lips. He pulled himself up slowly and tried to stand.

'Argh!' his pained scream echoed around the shaft as his leg gave way beneath him. He felt the bone and immediately knew that things weren't where they were meant to be. Looking about, he realised he still had his day pack with him.

At least there was a full canteen of water and some food. He pulled himself across the dirt floor to his bag and opened it, knowing that if he was going to have any chance of survival he had to ration his supplies – at least until he was strong enough to haul himself back up the ladder to the car.

This wasn't part of the plan. To die in a hole in the ground in the middle of Hope Springs. Although there was a certain irony to it, given he'd heard his own father had dropped dead of a heart attack in the western paddock. This wasn't how it was going to end. The time was finally here to find that mythical reef and put things right.

Chapter 26

'What a day,' Millie sighed as she climbed into bed. 'I can't believe that Lawrence was bitten by a snake. I hope the press doesn't find out, or Coober Pedy hospital won't know what hit them.'

'Stop talking,' Jacinta ordered. She pulled the covers over her head.

'It's a long way for the paparazzi to come,' Alice-Miranda said as she rummaged around in her suitcase looking for the book she'd brought to read. 'Millie, you didn't happen to grab anything from my bag today, did you?'

'Not me. Why?' the girl asked.

'It looks like everything's been moved,' Alice-Miranda replied.

'Is anything missing?' Larry asked. She'd crawled into her bottom bunk and was propped up on one elbow watching Alice-Miranda. Junie had already made herself at home on the end of the bed, with Rusty lying in the doorway.

The child located the book, which she was sure had been tucked down the right-hand side, but was now at the bottom. She frowned at the way her clothes were folded too – Shilly had long ago taught Alice-Miranda how to pack a bag neatly, but this looked as if it had been done by someone with extensive training in the art of garment origami.

'That does seem strange but I think everything's there,' Alice-Miranda said, as she climbed up onto the top bunk and switched on the reading lamp above her head.

'Speaking of strange – that Sprocket's a bit of a weird one,' Larry mused. 'Doesn't seem to remember if he's Arthur or Martha. Does he have a car or doesn't he, and where is it and how did it get here? He's all over the shop.'

'Total nutter,' Millie agreed. 'But at least he's entertaining, and that spag bol wasn't bad.'

'Sprocket!' Alice-Miranda gasped and sat bolt upright. 'Do you think he could have been looking in my bag?'

'Why would he do that?' Millie asked.

'He was pretty keen to get that piece of paper back,' Larry said.

'That's creepy,' Millie said. 'How would he know that you had it? Unless he was watching us when we stopped to look at the car?'

Alice-Miranda agreed. 'Even though he really didn't seem to know what it was or where he'd got it from in the first place.'

'And remember when he asked to use the bathroom?' Larry mused. 'First of all he said he knew where it was, then he backtracked. I think he'd already been in the house for sure. I wonder what else he's been into. I don't think we'll tell Mum too much – she gets a bit paranoid about blow-ins. We've had a few odd visitors over the years, but the worst was last spring. Dad and Ralph chased a couple of blokes off, and they made Hayden and me and Mum and Molly and Rosie and the kids hide in the cellar until they were gone. Ralph said he didn't like the look of them – he caught them poking around in the sheds and they were asking far too many questions that didn't seem to have anything to do with their alleged trip through the outback. They had a couple of bad-tempered hunting dogs in cages on their ute as well – Dad didn't want Rusty getting into trouble with them.'

From beneath the duvet there was a muffled sound. 'Thtop sthpeaking!'

'Sorry, Jacinta,' Larry said. 'I didn't mean to scare you. Just so you know, those guys left and we've never seen them again, and that's the only time we've ever really had any total weirdos on the property – apart from Sprocket, but I don't think he's dangerous. Just barking mad.'

Jacinta huffed and settled down again.

'I wish we could find the other half of that page – then we'd know for certain what it was,' Millie said.

Alice-Miranda threw the covers back. 'Anyone want to have another look in the study with me?'

'Sure,' Millie said, and Larry agreed, but Jacinta was either asleep or not interested as she didn't reply. The girls tiptoed out of the room and down the hallway.

Junie and Rusty stayed put.

Alice-Miranda flicked on the study light and looked around. 'We've already checked those ledgers up there.' She thought about the diary she'd returned to its hiding spot and felt a twinge in her stomach. She wasn't sure if it was guilt that she'd learned things she wished she hadn't, but it didn't sit well. Like an undigested French fry.

'What about this?' Larry pulled a brown leather-bound book from the shelves in the middle of the room. It was a large volume, landscape in shape and at least forty centimetres wide.

'Looks interesting,' Millie said as Larry laid the tome across the desk and opened the first page. There was a lot of swirly script, which Millie began to read aloud.

'Survey of Hope Springs Station, 1897,' she said. 'Maybe we're onto something here.'

The book contained a lot about the size of the place and the terrain, including prominent land-marks and the division of paddocks. There was some information about where the house was situated and the number of dwellings – of which there were quite a few more than currently existed.

Alice-Miranda looked on eagerly as the girls turned the page to find a hand-drawn map of the area immediately surrounding the homestead. The next page showed the yards and the sheds.

A board creaked on the veranda outside and Alice-Miranda's attention was diverted to the window. She could have sworn she saw a shadow, but maybe it was her imagination.

Millie glanced up too. 'What was that?'

'Just the house. This place makes so many noises,' Larry said. 'Some days, the tin roof expands and contracts to the point you'd swear there was a troop of tap-dancing goannas up there.'

Alice-Miranda and Millie grinned at each other, imagining the toe-tapping lizards.

Larry turned the pages slowly, carefully checking each one. The book was full of more maps and descriptions of paddocks and fencing. They were almost to the end when Millie let out a yelp and jumped into the air.

'What's the matter?' Alice-Miranda turned to the girl.

'Junie,' Millie panted, and pointed at the cat, who had padded silently into the room and curled her tail around Millie's bare leg, startling her.

Alice-Miranda reached down and picked the ginger puss up, cradling her in her arms like a baby. Junie purred loudly and rewarded the girl with a lick to the side of her face.

'I hope she doesn't have worms,' Millie grimaced. 'Mum always tells me off when the cats on the farm at home lick me.'

Alice-Miranda hoped so too. She'd wash her face before they went back to bed just to be sure. The girls reached the end of the book without any success.

'So much for that then,' Larry said. Millie returned it to the shelf and noticed another similar volume.

'Looks like there's a second one,' the girl said, and carried it over.

Larry turned the pages carefully again, wishing they would find something. She'd almost reached the end when their patience was rewarded.

'This is it!' Alice-Miranda stared at the torn sheet. 'I'm sure that it must be the other half.'

The page had been ripped down the middle, leaving a thin, ragged edge. 'If only we still had the page I gave back to Mr Sprocket, we could check. What does it say there?' She pointed at the writing on the facing page.

Neither Millie nor Larry could read the ornate script. Alice-Miranda peered in closely.

'The water on the table boasts a colourful feast, where Hope Springs eternal beneath a hungry rusty beast,' the girl read. 'Is it a riddle?'

'It sounds like one,' Larry said.

'What do you think it means?' Millie asked, the words coming out wrapped in a yawn.

'That there,' Larry pointed at the map. 'I think that's the boab tree. It's native to the Kimberley region in Western Australia, but somehow we have one growing in this paddock about a hundred kilometres from the homestead. Apparently, our great-great-grandfather had a fence built around it so that it couldn't be damaged by the stock, since it was considered so unusual. Molly says that the boab has all sorts of medicinal value. We haven't been out there for a long time.'

'Is there anything else that you recognise?' Millie asked.

Larry shook her head and rubbed her eyes. 'I'm too tired to think any more. Maybe we can work it out in the morning.'

Alice-Miranda felt a shiver of exhaustion run through her body. She set Junie down on the table.

'We're much more likely to solve it after we've had some sleep,' the girl said. They left the book open on the desk. Junie leapt down and followed them back to bed.

No one noticed the shadow on the front veranda, or heard the man enter the room through the unlocked French doors. He flicked on a torch and looked around, but he didn't have to search far, having overheard the girls' conversation. Now he had exactly what he needed.

Chapter 27

'You're not as useless as I thought,' the fellow said, glaring at Sprocket as he was presented with the other half of the map. 'Didn't think to get some sticky tape did you, so I could put it back together? And what's this red blob here? Better not be your blood, old timer.'

'Bolognaise sauce,' Sprocket replied. 'And who are you to be calling me "old timer". You must be sixty-five if you're a day.'

'That's none of your business. I'm glad you had something tasty for dinner,' he said sarcastically. He motioned at the empty tins of baked beans which he'd eaten cold and had been suffering the consequences of ever since.

'That explains the air in here.' Sprocket sniffed and screwed up his nose.

The man let one rip, then smirked. 'Smells like sunshine to me.'

Sprocket gagged. More like rotten egg gas. He may have lived on his own a long time, but he prided himself on behaving in a manner that would have made his old mum proud, unlike this fellow who quite likely *had* been raised by dingoes.

'I'm curious about something,' Sprocket said. 'How did you know Alice-Miranda had the map, and why did you leave your car on the side of the road with the door open?'

'Urgent call of nature. I had a bad chilli dog in Coober Pedy and it caught up with me in a hurry. If they'd stepped a few metres further they'd have seen me behind the mulga tree – it was just lucky I spotted them first and kept out of sight,' Wally replied. 'Didn't fancy being caught with my pants down. And I didn't need any nosey tourists asking questions.'

'That's funny. I told the kids much the same story. So what's the plan then?' Sprocket asked. 'I imagine you'll be keen to get wherever you're going. I'll just stay here and look after the kids until their parents return.'

The man frowned. 'Ah, no. You can't stay here. I need a labourer and, while you might be old, you're a wiry little ferret. You're coming with me.'

'But I thought you said that if I got you what you wanted, you'd let me go.' Sprocket swallowed hard, his Adam's apple practically lodging in his throat.

'I did. But I didn't say when. Besides, you told those kids that ute belonged to you. Would seem mighty suspicious if it just disappeared overnight and you were safe and sound here,' the man said, sitting down at the old laminex table to pore over the map and the riddle that went with it. Wherever that ute goes, you go with it – until I say you don't.'

Sprocket turned around and peered out the window into the starry sky.

'What am I supposed to tell the kids then?' he said.

'Nothing,' the bloke grinned. 'We'll be gone before they get up.'

'They'll think I'm a thief.' Sprocket's jaw flapped open.

'Better you than me,' the fellow said. 'Now, clear out these cupboards and go and see what else you can find.'

'What if I wake the kids?' Sprocket said.

The man looked at Sprocket and shook his head. 'Not in the main house, you dopey sod. Next door in the empty place.'

Sprocket felt sick. Lying and thieving didn't sit well with him at all. And on top of worrying whether he'd ever find his way back home again, he'd been thinking about Dan. Where was he? He wouldn't have left Junie. Something had happened to the silly old coot. Sprocket just hoped it wasn't fatal.

Alice-Miranda was woken by the sound of the phone ringing. She rolled over and looked down at the digital clock on the bedside cabinet, stunned to see that it was half past nine. The girls were all still asleep and, given the ringing hadn't stopped, she presumed the boys were too. Junie jumped down from Larry's bed and let out a hungry meow.

Alice-Miranda scrambled to the floor and hurried through the kitchen and into the pantry, where she picked up the handset.

'Good morning, Hope Springs,' she said. 'Alice-Miranda speaking.'

'Hello sweetheart. How are you all,' came the voice of Hugh.

'Hello Daddy, we're fine. Everyone's had a very late sleep in. I think we were all exhausted.'

Her father updated her on Lawrence's condition. He was getting stronger, but the doctors were keen to keep him under observation for another day or so.

'Will Uncle Barnaby be back later today?' the child asked, presuming that her father would stay with her uncle until he was healthy enough to return.

'I expect so. He'll fly back as soon as he can,' Hugh replied.

'Okay, Daddy. Don't worry about us. We're fine here.' She twirled a long curl around her finger while her father passed on information from Barnaby about the arrival of the cattle truck, which would be out soon to pick up the stock they'd mustered yesterday. They didn't have to do anything, he assured her. The driver and his offsider would load them.

'I'll let Larry and Hayden know. Speak to you later. Give Uncle Lawrence our love. Lucas and Jacinta were particularly upset about the snake bite, so I'll be glad to tell them that he's improved and is only staying for observation,' the child said. 'Love you.' And with that she hung up.

Alice-Miranda picked up a box of Weet-Bix on her way out of the pantry. She found a bowl in the cupboard and got the milk from the fridge.

Junie padded into the room and meowed.

'Sorry, kitty. Would you like some breakfast too?' the girl asked, and returned to the pantry where she located a tin of cat food that would have been stocked for Simba. It wasn't long before the two of them were eating in companionable silence. A few minutes later, Hayden appeared in the doorway.

'Gosh, we never sleep in this late,' the boy said as he grabbed a bowl from the cupboard and got himself some cereal too. 'Have you seen Sprocket this morning?'

Alice-Miranda shook her head. 'Might go and have a look after I get dressed. Daddy called and said Uncle Lawrence is doing well, but they want him to remain in hospital under observation for another day or so. Daddy's going to stay with him, but your father should be home sometime this morning in the helicopter and the truck's due shortly . . .' Her sentence was cut short by the arrival of the road train rumbling up the drive.

'Oh, I forgot about that,' Hayden said. He shovelled the last spoonful of cereal into his mouth and jumped up. 'I'd better get out there. Hopefully it's one of the regular drivers and he'll know what's what.'

'I'll get changed,' Alice-Miranda said, and dumped her breakfast bowl on the edge of the sink. In the sleep-out, she found Millie and the others awake and in various stages of dress. She put on her clothes and rushed out to the back veranda, where she grabbed her boots and hat and headed out to help Hayden.

As she charged up the driveway to the yards she realised Sprocket's white ute was missing. She wondered where he could have gone, given the nearest shops were over four hours' drive away and he'd promised to stay until the others returned. Perhaps he'd just moved it round the back of the sheds or something – but why was anyone's guess. While Sprocket was easily distracted, she didn't think he'd simply abandon them.

Chapter 28

Millie swatted at the flies, which seemed to have swarmed into mini tornadoes while the cattle were being loaded.

The children gave Bert and his offsider, Jase, a wave as the road train lurched forward on its long journey to the South Australian Livestock Exchange, about an hour north-west of Adelaide. They wouldn't get there until the early hours of the following morning, but at least there were two of them to share the driving.

It had taken almost two hours to herd the five-hundred head of cattle onto the four trailers. Bert and Jase did most of the heavy lifting, with some help from Hayden and Larry. The men had been shocked to hear that one of the station guests was in hospital recovering from a snake bite. Jase then shared several close calls of his own, including a recent run-in with an inland taipan, which didn't do much to settle Millie's nerves.

She and Alice-Miranda had busied themselves making tea and sandwiches for the men, while Lucas was on hand to fetch and carry as required. Jacinta had begged off with a headache and was spending the day in front of the television with a cold flannel on her forehead. Millie wasn't sure if she was genuinely unwell, or still stricken about what had happened to Lawrence, but given Jase's stories it was probably for the best.

Earlier, Alice-Miranda had done a lap of the sheds and outbuildings to see if Sprocket's car had been moved somewhere else, then she did a quick check of the dongas to see if perhaps he'd fallen asleep inside, but he was nowhere to be found.

'Good job, everyone,' Hayden said now as they headed for the homestead. They all had a speedy wash before cool drinks were dispensed, and an Anzac slice that Larry had taken out of the freezer the night before was consumed with gusto.

Alice-Miranda looked in on Jacinta, who was snoozing on the lounge with Junie curled into her tummy. She walked back to the kitchen without waking the pair.

'Has anyone seen Sprocket?' Alice-Miranda asked.

The others all shook their heads.

'His ute's gone,' Millie said. 'So much for him looking after us until Barnaby got back.'

Larry scoffed. 'Few roos loose in the top paddock, you might say.'

'He'll probably turn up and tell us he just went for a drive in the countryside or something,' Hayden said.

Alice-Miranda reached for another piece of Anzac slice. Sprocket was an odd one, that's for sure.

'Do you want to see if we can make any more sense of that map?' she asked.

Millie explained to Hayden and Lucas what they'd discovered the previous night.

'Sure,' the boys replied, and the children made their way to the study at the front of the house.

'Didn't you leave that open?' Millie pointed at the now-closed book.

Alice-Miranda frowned and nodded.

Larry turned the pages, looking for the torn section. She thought she was in about the right place when she spotted the jagged edges close to the spine.

'Our half is gone!' she declared.

'What do you mean it's gone?' Millie said. 'It was there when we went to bed.'

There was a short silence until the children all had the same thought at once.

'Sprocket!' the children exclaimed.

'He must have come for the map,' Alice-Miranda said. 'He was just pretending to be in the neighbourhood and that's why he was so desperate to get the other half back.'

'But how would he know about it?' Millie said, shaking her head.

Hayden was pacing up and down the length of the room, while Lucas was deep in thought.

'It had an "X" on it, didn't it?' Lucas said.

'Yes,' Alice-Miranda said. 'The bit I found on the way out here did – but that's the part I gave to Sprocket.'

'He was so evasive about what it was when you asked him yesterday,' Larry said.

'It's got to be the treasure map. Molly must be right about the legend of the opal deposit somewhere on Hope Springs,' Hayden said.

'Well, if it's true and there is a fortune out there, it's on our land, so technically he'd be stealing it,' Larry said.

Alice-Miranda pointed at the riddle on the facing page and brought their attention back to the book. 'Okay – given you said that the boab tree was in the top left corner, we know that the map covers the area about one hundred kilometres to the north of the homestead, and the "X" was to the east of that. So what could this mean?' She recited the riddle for everyone.

Hayden sat down in the swivel chair and spun around, tapping his finger against his chin.

'There's no surface water out that way at all,' he said.

'But we have water because it comes from the bores,' Larry said.

'The water table!' Hayden said. 'But it's well below ground level.'

Lucas had perched on one of the lower rungs of the library ladder. 'The colourful feast has got to be the opals.'

'What about the hungry rusty beast?' Millie said. 'Are there any old trucks or cars out there?'

Larry slumped against the desk. 'Lots. There's abandoned tractors and farm equipment and some cars and trucks that I've seen when we've been going round the property. They're spread out for miles – it would take forever to find them all.'

'We don't need to find them *all*,' Alice-Miranda grinned. 'We just need to find the right one.'

'What are you doing?' Jacinta appeared in the doorway and yawned widely.

'Are you okay?' Millie asked the girl. She felt bad for having given her friend a bit of a hard time since they'd set out on the trip.

'Fine. Hungry, actually. Is there anything to eat?' Jacinta asked.

Millie offered to go and make her a sandwich while everyone else brought the girl up to speed on what they'd discovered.

Millie looked out the louvres on the back veranda on the way to the kitchen and noticed a cloud of dust swirling behind the sheds.

'Hey!' she called. 'I think Sprocket's back.'

There was a stampede as the rest of the children ran down the hallway to join her. But the dust kept swirling as if the vehicle was driving straight past. Alice-Miranda grabbed her boots and pulled them on, then charged out into the backyard and through the gate to the sheds. She ran around the corner just in time to see the white ute hurtling away along the road past the cattle yards.

Hayden was right behind her.

'He's gone again,' the girl puffed. Alice-Miranda stared into the distance.

She was thinking about everything that had happened the day before when she remembered something unusual that she'd seen when she'd gone looking for Sprocket earlier. 'Come with me,' Alice-Miranda said, and grabbed the boy's hand, pulling him towards the staff dongas.

She ran up the veranda steps and into the first of the huts.

'What are we looking for?' Hayden asked as Alice-Miranda pushed open the door.

'Sprocket said that he was going to sleep in his swag outside last night, but when I came looking earlier I saw that the bed was all mussed up in here.'

'I did offer for him to sleep inside, so he could have changed his mind,' Hayden replied.

'I imagine he does that quite often, but what about those?' She pointed at three empty tins of baked beans sitting on the sink.

'Sprocket said last night at dinner that he was glad not to have to eat baked beans as they were his least favourite food.' Hayden nodded. 'Do you think someone else is with him then?'

Alice-Miranda peered into the rubbish bin and found three cigarette stubs.

'Does anyone who lives here smoke?' she asked.

Hayden shook his head. 'None of Molly's family do.'

'And neither does Sprocket either. He told us he didn't when we were at his dugout,' the girl explained.

'Alice-Miranda!' Millie called.

'We're in here,' Hayden yelled. Millie and Larry raced up the stairs and into the donga next door by mistake. But it was just as well they did.

'Hey, guys, where are you? You need to see this!' Larry called.

Alice-Miranda and Hayden ran to find them. Jacinta and Lucas were there now too.

'Whoa, this place is filthy,' Hayden said as the dust particles danced on the sunbeam that streamed through the back window.

'Not important,' Larry said and pointed at the dark red laminex table top.

Written in dust across the centre were the words, 'Kids, help! He's going to ki.. me. The map. Sprock . . .'

The last few words were smudged almost as if he'd rubbed them out, but the message was clear.

'Sprocket's been kidnapped!' Alice-Miranda declared.

'And I don't think whoever has him is planning to kiss him, do you?' Millie said.

'No wonder he couldn't describe the map properly – he came to get it for someone else,' Jacinta said.

'I didn't look in here earlier – only next door. Then I just ran along calling Sprocket's name and opening and closing the doors. Oh my goodness.

I don't think that is his white ute after all,' Alice-Miranda said.

'Come on, we need to go after them,' Larry said.

A row of frown lines took up residence on Jacinta's forehead. 'What? Out there – again? With all the snakes and the dinosaur lizards and the pterodactyls. Count me out.'

'Seriously,' Millie started, then noticed a fierce look from Alice-Miranda. 'Seriously, it's a great idea if you stay here and look after the house and Junie and wait until Barnaby gets back. I imagine he shouldn't be too long if he's coming by chopper . . . And we should probably let your father and Hugh know what's happening too.'

Jacinta thought some more. 'But then I'll be here on my own.' She stared at Lucas hoping that he'd volunteer to stay behind.

Lucas looked at her and shrugged. 'I think I should go with the others. Sprocket needs our help.'

'We have to get some things together,' Larry said. The children hurried back to the house and made plans.

Chapter 29

It was just after one o'clock when the children left the homestead on their search for Sprocket. They were armed with maps recreated from what Larry, Alice-Miranda and Millie could remember about the two halves they'd discovered. They also had the riddle with them and were on the lookout for rusty metal objects.

They'd divided up the jobs for their preparation – the three girls were on map making, Hayden was on food, Lucas was on water bottles and compasses, and it had been Jacinta's job to sort the two-way radios. They'd got everything together in record time.

Alice-Miranda had tried to call her father, but he hadn't answered and she decided it was probably best not to leave a message – he'd only worry. Hayden couldn't get through to Barnaby, which meant he was probably flying. He didn't leave a message either. Instead, Alice-Miranda wrote the men a note, in case they arrived before the children, and taped it to the back door.

Now, Larry and Hayden rode the trail bikes while Millie went with Alice-Miranda on one four-wheeler and Lucas and Jacinta doubled on another. Right before they'd been about to leave, Jacinta had changed her mind and decided she'd rather be with her friends than at the homestead with a demanding ginger cat and the prospect of a long afternoon alone. Rusty was with them too, much to Junie's dismay.

The children rode side by side across the dry paddock, keeping an eye out for tyre tracks. The boab was at least two hours north by motorbike, but they headed east of the tree, hoping that the spot marked with an 'X' would be on their trajectory.

It was hot and dusty, with endless miles of mulga trees, scrub and red dirt. They saw emus aplenty and a huge mob of camels – at least two dozen – which Hayden took note of. The beasts were in plague proportions in the outback at the moment, and did a great deal of damage to the land and fences. The group rode for over an hour and a half before Millie spotted some tracks.

She tapped Alice-Miranda on the shoulder and pointed. The girl brought the four-wheeler to a stop. Millie dug about in the backpack she and Alice-Miranda were sharing and pulled out the two-way radio, but when she went to switch it on the signal was weak and she couldn't get any volume.

Fortunately, the others had noticed the girls were missing and turned back.

'Sorry – the radio battery seems really low,' Millie said. 'We found some tracks.'

Jacinta rolled her eyes. 'Give me a look,' she said. Millie handed over the device and the girl shook her head. 'I don't understand. I got all the radios out and the recharged batteries and . . .' Jacinta's face crumpled. 'Oh no. I meant to change them over and then when I decided to come I raced off to get ready and I didn't do it. All the charged

batteries are still sitting in the pantry. I'm so sorry –
I'm an idiot.'

'We'll go back,' Lucas suggested. 'And you're
not an idiot.'

'No,' Larry said. 'It'll take too long.'

Jacinta looked ashen. 'It's okay,' Millie said.
She felt sorry for the girl. Clearly she hadn't meant
for this to happen.

'We'll be fine,' Hayden said. 'We just won't use
the radios unless it's absolutely necessary. Everyone
switch them off.'

They did as they were told, noting that the
batteries all had less than half an hour's life left in
them. Thankfully it was something.

Minutes later, the children were congregated
near the wheel tracks in the dirt.

'They're definitely fresh,' Hayden said. 'This
soft soil would have been covered by now if they'd
been more than a day or so old, especially with
all those camels around. This paddock has lots of
stock too.'

The kids followed the trail, which continued
on a north easterly path for miles.

'There!' Alice-Miranda shouted. But it wasn't
the white ute that she'd spotted.

In the distance, the blades of a rusty windmill poked out above a large clump of mulga trees.

'Could that be the rusty beast in the riddle?' she said.

'That would be pretty lucky if it was,' Millie replied. 'And I'm not sure if you'd call a windmill hungry.'

The group slowed down as they approached a rocky outcrop. Hayden braked hard and held his hand up to stop the rest of them. He rode his bike behind the boulders and the others followed.

'What is it?' Larry asked as they all killed their engines.

'I think I saw someone,' he said.

The children climbed to the top of the red rocks and lay on their stomachs to get a better view. The windmill was still at least a half a kilometre away, which was just as well. Hopefully, whoever was out there hadn't heard them approaching.

Larry pulled a pair of binoculars from her backpack and had a look.

'White ute!' she exclaimed. 'On the other side of the trees.'

She passed the binoculars to Alice-Miranda beside her.

'It looks like a campsite. There's a tarp strung up, and one of those portable gas stoves,' the child said.

'What are we going to do?' Lucas asked. 'We need a plan to rescue Sprocket.'

Millie bit her lip. 'I think an ambush would work best. All of us arriving at once. Come at them from four sides, then Sprocket can make a quick getaway while the other guy's distracted.'

'What if he's armed?' Alice-Miranda said.

Jacinta looked at her and rolled her eyes. 'Sprocket won't shoot us. We're rescuing him.'

There were a few giggles. 'It's not Sprocket we're worried about, Jacinta,' Lucas said.

Her mouth formed a perfect 'O' as she realised what the boy meant.

No one had thought of that until now, but there was a fairly high likelihood that the person who had taken Sprocket had a weapon. Even Barnaby usually carried a rifle on the motorbike with him as a precautionary measure for livestock issues. Given the local vet was over four hours' drive away, sometimes euthanasia was the only humane thing to do.

'Even if he does have a gun, he can't fire at all of us at the same time,' Alice-Miranda said.

'Especially if we surprise them. And maybe we could make a lot of noise too. Hayden do you still have those flares we took when we were searching for Matilda?'

'Yes,' the boy said. 'That would be a shock if we let them off.'

The others agreed. They had to try.

A shadow momentarily blocked out the sun. Jacinta looked skywards and screamed when she saw a creature with a small furry animal clutched in its talons.

'The pterodactyls are back. Come on, let's go!' she urged.

'Jacinta, they're not pterodactyls,' Alice-Miranda called after her, but the girl was having none of it.

'I don't believe you,' she said, scrambling back down the rocks to the four-wheeler.

Lucas looked at the others with upturned palms.

'We tried,' Millie said.

Minutes later the plan was ready. Hayden would head further out and approach the camp from the north, while the others would fan left and right and Larry would stay on track from the south. The children would arrive at the camp simultaneously from all sides. Hopefully Sprocket would realise it was a distraction and make a run for it. He could get a double back with either Hayden or Larry – whoever was nearest to him.

The mosquito buzz of the four-stroke engines zipped towards the campsite until they were only metres away.

A dog began to bark. They couldn't see it properly, but Rusty jumped off the back of Larry's bike and ran into the camp, wagging his tail and creating chaos.

'Rusty!' the girl yelled, but the dog wasn't listening.

'Oi, get out of here, you mongrel!' a voice yelled. A man walked into the clearing. He had bright red hair and wore a blue singlet, stubbies and a dusty pair of workboots with long grey socks.

Another fellow followed. He was hairy and tanned with a tattoo on his right bicep and a shock of dark curls. Neither of them was Sprocket.

The kids killed their engines and hopped off their bikes.

'G'day,' the tattooed bloke said to Larry with a nod. He had a steely gaze and didn't take his eyes off the girl.

'Hi,' Larry replied. 'Just wondering what you're doing out here. You do know this is private property?' She eyeballed the man. Alice-Miranda walked over and stood beside her. Millie stayed with the four-wheeler.

The red-haired fellow ran his tongue around his teeth and turned full circle, wondering why the kids had come from four different directions. 'Um, we were just camped for the night. On our way through to Oodnadatta.'

'Pretty early to have already set up camp and you're a long way from the road,' Hayden said, his brow furrowed. He walked further into the campsite and caught sight of the dog cage. Rusty was barking at the animal inside. It took a moment for the boy to realise that the occupant was no stranger. 'Blue Dog!' he called and ran to open the door and let her out. The animal jumped on him and licked his face, then took off with Rusty haring about like two long lost pals.

Hayden stood up. 'Where did you get the dog?' he demanded.

'It wandered into the campsite,' the hairy bloke replied.

'When?' Alice-Miranda asked.

'A few days . . .' the skinny fellow started, until he noticed his mate glaring.

'You said you were only camped here for tonight,' Lucas challenged.

'I meant a few hours . . .' the man corrected himself, but the kids weren't buying it.

'Sorry, sir, we haven't even been properly introduced yet. I'm Alice-Miranda Highton-Smith-Kennington-Jones, here visiting our good friends the Lewises who own this property, Hope Springs,' the child offered her hand to the two very surprised fellows. 'These are my friends.' She proceeded to name everyone and explain who lived here and who didn't. 'And you are?'

'I'm Muz,' the skinny bloke said with a grin, 'and he's Col.'

'Sheesh, way to go telling them our real names,' the bigger bloke mumbled to himself softly, but Alice-Miranda caught it.

'Why wouldn't you tell us your real names?' she asked. 'Unless you have something to hide.'

'Don't know what you're talking about, miss,' the man said. 'I didn't say a word.'

Lucas had wandered around the camp and

noticed there seemed to a big pile of tin cans and other rubbish. Certainly more than one morning's worth.

'We were wondering if you've seen anyone out here today. They were driving a white ute with a dog cage on the back,' Larry said, her eyes drilling holes in the pair.

They both shook their heads.

'Haven't seen a soul,' Col said. 'Although we noticed some dust swirling to the east a little while back. Thought it must have been a willy willy, but out here it's always hard to tell.'

'Okay,' Larry said. 'We'll be taking the dog with us. She belongs to our neighbours.'

'Oh, that's good to know. Appreciate if you could. She's been eating us out of house and home,' Muz said.

'I thought you said she only arrived today,' Hayden frowned. These guys had to be the worst liars he'd ever come across.

'Yeah, but she was hungry,' the other bloke said. 'Reckon she would have cleaned us out if we'd kept opening tins for her.'

Alice-Miranda had a strange feeling that there was a lot more to the story than these two were letting on. She looked closely at the camp and their swags and the ute. She nudged Larry and raised her chin towards the tray. The tailgate was down and they could see inside.

Larry let out a tiny gasp. Both girls had noticed the same thing. A toolbox with Saxby Downs written on the side.

She mouthed the word 'water' to Alice-Miranda.

Alice-Miranda's eyes widened. 'You think they're tampering with the bores?' she whispered, remembering what Hugh had told her while explaining what the men had found just before Lawrence was bitten. They needed to play this cool or they risked having the pair take off, never to be seen again – or worse if they realised the kids knew what they were up to.

'I think we should call the police,' Larry whispered. 'Get Millie to take a picture.'

Alice-Miranda nodded.

'Well, it was very nice to meet you, Col and Muz, but we should get going. It's a long way back to the homestead,' Alice-Miranda said.

The men gave a wave. She and Larry went to leave when it was Alice-Miranda's turn to gasp. Slung over one of the camp chairs was a blanket – the same as the one Matilda had been wrapped in when she was found in the machinery shed.

She spun back around. 'You didn't happen to come across a little girl out here a few days ago?' Alice-Miranda asked, watching their reactions carefully.

'A little girl!' Muz exclaimed. 'Why would a little girl be out here wandering about on her own? That's not very safe now, is it?'

Anyone would have thought he was auditioning for a part in a soap opera, given his horrible overacting.

'She was lost but someone brought her to the homestead at Hope Springs. The police are very keen to speak to whoever it was,' the child said.

Col's eyes didn't leave the ground. He shook his head. 'Nope, told ya we only just got here this morning. Haven't seen any kids out here except you lot.'

Alice-Miranda didn't believe a word of it. And neither did the others.

'Is she okay?' Muz asked. 'The little girl.'

'She's fine,' Alice-Miranda replied. 'She's been chatting away telling everyone about her big adventure.'

The other kids turned and stared, wondering what she was playing at.

'But that little girl's de . . .' Muz started, then clamped his hand over his mouth.

'Gotcha!' Alice-Miranda pointed her finger at him. 'I knew you weren't telling the truth. That blanket is the same as the one Matilda was lying on when she was found. Uncle Barnaby said that it hadn't come from their property.'

Hayden grinned. Alice-Miranda was so smart. He would have never thought to trap them like that.

The man gulped and looked like a five-year-old who'd just been caught with his hand in the cookie jar. 'I swear, we didn't hurt her or anything. We gave her some food and took her home,' he babbled.

Alice-Miranda drew herself up taller. 'What I don't understand is why you didn't just bring her to the door.'

The last thing Muz and Col needed was to have the police pay them a visit. But maybe if they explained the situation – well, their imaginary version of events – to the kids, they'd keep it to themselves and that'd be the end of it. Because if the police got involved, undoubtedly one thing would lead to another and the two of them would be in a mess of trouble.

'Would you kids like some tea and a biscuit?' Col asked. 'We'll tell you the whole story.' He looked at Muz with a glare that said he was planning to do all the talking.

Alice-Miranda whispered to Larry. 'Let's hear what they have to say for themselves. They're not the sharpest pair, but they'll be worried about us getting the police if we let on that we know what they've been up to – apart from the fact that they found Matilda and didn't tell anyone.'

Larry called the others over to her while Col boiled the billy on the camp stove and Muz set about finding mugs. Alice-Miranda offered to help while Larry explained to the others in hushed tones exactly who she and Alice-Miranda thought they were and what they were planning to do about it.

Chapter 30

The men admitted they'd been camped there for a few days, but their story was surprising.

They said they were hiding out from someone they'd offended at one of the roadhouses on the way from Alice Springs. Even though they swore they hadn't done anything wrong, the owner said he was getting the police after them, so they decided to lay low for a while on their way up north.

'Which roadhouse?' Millie asked.

'Um, Cadney . . .' Col began, but at the exact same time Muz chimed in with, 'Kulgera.'

Col glared at Muz. 'Yeah, that's the one.'

'We've been there,' Jacinta said.

'So you had a fight with Wally and his wife, Sharon,' Millie said. 'They're an interesting couple.'

'She knows everything about everyone,' Larry said. 'And isn't afraid to share it.'

'Yeah, great,' Col said, though pursed lips. Of all the roadhouses, Muz had to mention one the kids were familiar with. Boofhead.

'So what happened?' Lucas said.

The two men exchanged nervous glances. 'Um, she accused me of not paying for my beer, which I absolutely did and so I got a bit hot under the collar and we had words,' Col said. 'Nothing really.'

Muz leaned forward and decided to add some colour to the story, much to Col's horror.

'Well, there was more to it than that, wasn't there, mate?' he said.

'No, there wasn't,' Col snapped.

'Yeah, there was.' Muz nodded, a dopey grin plastered across his face. 'Sharon came at Col and threw a left hook and he went down like a bag of spuds, so I leapt up on the counter and it was on for young and old, and the place got properly busted up,' he blurted.

'You finished?' Col glared at his friend again. 'Can't just leave things alone, can you, mate?'

Muz shrugged, wondering what he'd done wrong. He'd always been taught never to let the truth get in the way of a good story and he was particularly enjoying making this one up.

The children looked at one another.

'You know violence never fixed anything,' Jacinta said.

Millie nibbled her lip to suppress a giggle because she knew Jacinta hadn't always subscribed to that theory.

'Yeah, we know, but that's what happened, and then when the little one wandered into the campsite we both sort of panicked. Didn't want any trouble with the cops, so that's why we left her in the shed,' Col said.

'But we fed her and made sure she was okay,' Muz chimed in, garnering himself yet another glare from Col.

'And that's it,' Larry said.

'Yeah, what else would there be?' Muz said with a frown.

'Anyway, we'll be off tomorrow morning. Won't be round these parts again for a while,' Col said.

'Well, thank you for telling us the truth about Matilda,' Alice-Miranda said. 'We can pass that on to Sergeant Ted and the Darleys. It's a pity you don't have time to meet them. I'm sure they would have loved to be able to thank you for bringing her home.'

'We're glad that she was found. It's a dangerous place for a little kid out here,' Col mumbled.

'Thank you for the tea too,' Alice-Miranda said as she tipped the last of the dregs onto the ground beside her.

'You need to keep a lookout for that white ute we told you about before – with the dog cage. The man driving it could be dangerous. We think he's taken a friend of ours hostage,' Millie explained.

'Hostage!' Muz exclaimed. This place was a nightmare. The sooner they finished their job the better. The only reason they'd been at camp when the kids showed up was that they'd run out of parts and were waiting for the boss to drop some more. Hopefully he wouldn't arrive in the chopper anytime soon, or they'd really be in trouble.

'Why would the bloke take your friend?' Col asked.

'They're looking for something,' Millie said. 'Something under a rusty beast.'

Muz looked over at the windmill. 'Well, that old girl fits the description.'

The children turned their attention to the machinery.

'Does it still work?' Millie asked.

Muz and Col weren't about to tell her that it did. Better the children didn't know, given plugging the bore attached to the windmill would be their last job before they left the property.

The children all stood up and walked over to investigate. The windmill sat right beside another rocky outcrop.

'Hey, look at this,' Lucas called. He pointed between the stones to a gap almost big enough for a child to crawl through. 'What do you think? Should I take a look?'

'I wouldn't go in there. It's a perfect hideout for snakes,' Hayden said.

'Don't even talk about them!' Jacinta yelled, and made a run back to the four-wheeler where she climbed up to stand on the seat and stared out into the distance.

Larry grabbed a torch and lay down on her stomach to get a better look. She flicked the light on and shone it around. Sadly, there were no sparkles or twinkles. 'Just a bunch of old rocks, as far as I can tell.' There was disappointment in her voice. She didn't know what she was expecting. Maybe a dazzling cave full of opals – but that would have been too easy.

'Someone's coming,' Jacinta called. She could see a vehicle heading towards them in the distance, dust flying up behind. It was speeding from the east.

Alice-Miranda looked at Muz and Col, who didn't seem especially excited to have more visitors.

She and Lucas clambered to the top of the rocks beside the windmill. They could see it too.

'It's a white ute,' Lucas called back.

'You say this bloke's dangerous?' Col said.

'We don't know for sure, but he could be,' Hayden said.

'Maybe you kids should hide and see how things play out. If your friend is with them, then hopefully Col and I can secure his release,' Muz said.

'Geez, what are you, a New York detective or something?' Col looked at Muz and shook his head.

There was another rocky outcrop only about fifty metres to the west. If the children left now they'd be able to get there without being spotted, and then use their binoculars to keep an eye on things.

'Take your bikes, kids. Go!' Col ordered.

The children did as they were told, though not before they distracted the men long enough for Alice-Miranda to direct Millie to snap pictures of them and their ute – including the toolbox with Saxby Downs emblazoned on the side. At least the police could investigate what they'd been up to. A few minutes later, the children, along with Rusty and Blue Dog, were holed up behind the rocks, waiting to see what happened next.

Chapter 31

'There's no place like home, is there love,' Molly said to Ralph as the main homestead hove into view. But if they were hoping for a welcoming party, the pair was to be sorely disappointed.

'Place looks a bit quiet,' Ralph said as they turned the corner behind the big house and headed down the road to their home. 'Thought the kids would have been out to say hello, or at least Rusty'd be waggin' his tail for us.'

'If the silly old phone battery hadn't died days

ago, I could've called, but it still doesn't make sense that no one's been picking up the two-way. Unless something's happened,' Molly said. 'I knew I should have called before we left up north. I've got a bad feeling in my bones, Ralph Robinson. Something's off.'

Molly and Ralph had left their family and headed for home a week ago. Sam, Rosie and the kids were on their way too, a couple of days behind. Buddy had got himself a mustering job up north, but was due to be finished before the weekend.

Ralph pulled up at the front of their farm-house and the pair hopped out, stretching and creaking, complaining about their old bones and how long car trips didn't agree with either of them any more.

Molly walked around to the back door and into the kitchen, where she popped the kettle on.

When she walked into the pantry, her eyes grew wide. She looked about, scanning the empty shelves.

'Ralph!' the woman called to her husband, who was lugging their suitcases inside. 'Ralph, get in here.'

'What's the matter?' he called back.

'We've been robbed,' she yelled. He thundered down the hallway from the front door and met her in the kitchen.

'What did they take?' he asked, glancing about.

'Food, and lots of it,' she said, and stepped aside so he could see the storeroom. There were huge gaps in the tinned stocks, and most of the pasta and rice was missing. There wasn't a packet of biscuits left either. Ralph lifted the lid on the chest freezer to see that half their meat supplies had disappeared as well.

'Better head over and see if we can find Barnaby,' he said. Molly nodded. The idea that there had been strangers lurking about while they'd been gone didn't sit well. She did a quick check of the sitting room and the bedrooms, but it looked as if whoever had been there was only after food supplies.

'I'll come with you,' Molly said, following her husband.

The pair trekked down the winding driveway to the main homestead, where they were surprised at the back door by the note from Alice-Miranda and a bossy ginger cat.

Dan's eyes struggled open and he realised that he'd been dreaming again. It had happened a lot since the accident, and he was beginning to wonder what was even real.

The pain in his leg was making him feel nauseous and he was sweating up a storm. If he didn't get out of here soon, he never would. And given no one knew where he was, the likelihood of being rescued hadn't crossed his mind.

Dan let his thoughts wander. He never imagined his life would have turned out the way it did. He was meant to be a farmer, not a miner. Maybe if he'd been born fifty years later, things would have been different. But not back in the days when blurring the lines meant facing the consequences – and they had been more than he could bear. You couldn't help who you loved, and why should you. He'd spent a lifetime doing the only thing he knew that might make a difference, mining because he had to. And if he managed this one last payday, he could shuffle off the mortal coil knowing he had at least done some good in the world.

Chapter 32

'No!' Alice-Miranda wheezed as the driver of the white ute stepped out and was greeted by Col and Muz. She recognised the man immediately.

'What is it?' Millie demanded.

'I think it's Wally from the roadhouse!' she exclaimed.

'Maybe Muz and Col were telling the truth about the fight,' Millie said.

'I doubt it – they're a pair of terrible liars,' Larry said, but the fact that Wally was heading to their camp didn't bode well. Had Wally been searching for Col and Muz as well as the treasure all this time? And why had he kidnapped Sprocket? What did the miner have to do with any of this?

'Is Sprocket with him?' Larry asked urgently.

Alice-Miranda panned the binoculars around, but she couldn't see him. 'I don't think so – unless he's in the back of the ute.'

'Has Wally punched anyone yet?' Lucas asked.

The others looked at the boy quizzically.

'Well, you'd think if he was seeking revenge on Col and Muz, then he might come out swinging, given they said they'd made a mess of the bar,' the boy explained.

'True.' The others all nodded.

'It looks like they're having a chat,' Alice-Miranda said. 'And he just sat down and Muz passed him a mug.'

'Weird,' Millie said, then gasped. 'Oh my goodness. Do you think Muz and Col are working with Wally and we just gave them way too much information?'

'Maybe they're all in on the bore tampering and Saxby Downs is paying them to steal our water! What if the map had something to do with that and it's not about the opals?' Larry said, shaking her head.

Alice-Miranda frowned and set the binoculars down. 'There's something strange going on, that's for sure.'

'We need to get closer and see what that Wally guy is up to,' Larry said. 'And if we could find the map and take it back, then even better. Without it, he won't know where to look . . . for whatever it is he's looking for. Unless he thinks the windmill is the right spot?'

Alice-Miranda passed the binoculars to Hayden, who kept an eye on things for the next ten minutes or so.

'I vote we do some reconnaissance and check out his truck,' Larry said.

'I'll go,' Alice-Miranda offered.

'I'm not going into that camp again,' Jacinta whimpered. 'I didn't like Wally when we met him at the roadhouse and I can't imagine I'm going to like him any better now.'

'Fine,' Millie said. 'You can stay here with the dogs and send a signal if it looks like we're about to be caught.'

Jacinta sighed. That sounded like a lot of pressure. She wasn't especially keen on that idea either.

Larry bit her lip. 'We can't all go. We need to have at least three people here with the bikes in case we need rescuing,' Larry said.

The others all agreed.

'Okay, I'll stay,' Lucas volunteered.

Jacinta smiled at the boy. 'Thank you,' she mouthed.

The others all wanted to go, so they decided who would stay the only reasonable way they could. With a guessing game. Lucas scratched a number onto a rock out of sight for proof.

'Okay, whoever picks the right number is the loser and has to hang back with us,' Jacinta explained.

They got to three rounds before Larry lost with the number two. 'I thought you would have picked thirteen for sure,' she said.

'Way too obvious,' Lucas replied.

The children agreed that if they got into any trouble, a cooee would be the signal for the others to come for them on the bikes. And the same was to happen in reverse – if Lucas, Jacinta and Larry thought Alice-Miranda, Millie and Hayden were about to be caught, one of them would cooee too.

Alice-Miranda, Hayden and Millie crept from their hiding spot and wove their way through the scrawny shrubs until they reached the edge of Col and Muz's campsite. Crouching behind a cluster of rocks, they peered at the men, who certainly didn't look like mortal enemies. Wally was munching on a biscuit and sipping from his mug, though Muz wore a pinched expression and Col was pacing up and down.

'So what are you lads doin' out this way then?' Wal asked.

'Just passin' through,' Col said.

'Got some work if you're keen,' Wally said. 'Any good with a shovel and pick?'

'What are we digging for?' Muz asked.

'Treasure,' Wally said with a grin. He waved at a swarm of flies, then clamped his lips down on a stray, which disappeared inside his mouth. Wally took a gulp from his cup, swished it around and spat the tea, along with the fly, onto the ground beside him.

'He's gross,' Millie whispered.

'So where is this treasure?' Col asked.

'About ten feet away, if I have my directions right,' Wally said.

Muz glanced at Col. 'What's in it for us?'

'Let's just say if you help me find what I'm looking for, you'll have more money than you'll ever be able to spend,' the man replied.

'You don't have anyone else with you?' Col said.

'Yeah, but he's havin' a sleep in the back of the ute,' Wally said. 'Couldn't risk him running off so I gave him something, but he should be up soon.'

The children's eyes grew wide. Sprocket was right here.

'I've got an idea,' Hayden said. 'But we're going to have to move fast and you have to trust me. I know what I'm doing. I've been driving since I was six.'

Millie bit her lip as Hayden explained. What the boy was proposing sounded dangerous – and incredibly exciting. They needed to get a message to the others. She volunteered to go while Alice-Miranda kept watch and created a distraction.

Millie bolted back towards the rocky outcrop where the lookouts were hiding, while Hayden crept around to the first white ute – the one that belonged to Muz and Col. He reached in and took the keys at exactly the same time Alice-Miranda threw a rock, which thudded onto the dirt. The three fellows turned to look.

'Probably a roo – there was a big mob of them out here before,' Col said.

Moments later, Hayden was in the driver's seat of Wally's ute with Alice-Miranda beside him.

'Buckle up,' the boy said, and started the engine.

'What the heck!' Wally leapt from his camp chair and ran towards the vehicle.

Hayden grinned at the man as he reversed at top speed before slamming on the brakes and crunching the car into gear. 'Sorry, Sprocket.' He apologised to the man, who they assumed was asleep under the tarpaulin.

'Come back here, you little brats!' Wally shouted, then looked at Col and Muz. 'Don't just stand there, you idiots.' Wally raced over to the other ute and jumped into the driver's seat, Col hopping in beside him while Muz leapt up into the tray and grabbed the rollbar.

Wally reached for the ignition.

'Keys, where are the blasted keys?' he demanded.

'They were in there, I swear,' Col said. 'The kids must have taken them.'

The ping of two-stroke engines filled the air and the four motorbikes flew out from their hiding spot.

The convoy streamed across the desert, a plume of red dust filling the air. Rusty and Blue Dog were perched on the back of Millie's and Lucas's four-wheelers – thankfully used to this sort of travelling.

The children continued for at least five kilometres before Hayden brought the ute to a stop and the others caught up.

'Wow, that was incredible!' Millie panted. 'I don't think my heart's ever beat so fast.'

Larry pointed at the girl's mouth. 'Bugs.'

Millie ran her tongue over a smattering of dead insects that had been caught in her teeth. She used her finger to wipe them away, then grabbed a drink bottle and took a swig, spitting the menagerie onto the ground.

'Mr Sprocket!' Alice-Miranda called as she jumped out of the passenger seat and lifted the tarp. She found tools and boxes of tinned food and two eskies in the tray, but the man wasn't there.

'Oh no, Wally was lying,' the girl gasped.

'He could have murdered him and left him for the pterodactyls to pick over his bones,' Jacinta said, then began to cry. 'I hate the outback. I want to go home.'

'Is there any blood in there?' Lucas asked, putting an arm around Jacinta.

Alice-Miranda shook her head. 'I can't see any.'

'Sprocket's way too smart to let an idiot like Wally do him in,' Millie said. 'I bet he escaped.'

Larry's attention turned to the other matter at hand. 'Did you find the maps?'

Alice-Miranda nodded and ran back to fetch them from in the centre console.

She laid the two half pages on the open tailgate side by side, looking at the whole picture for the first time.

'Wally said the treasure was at the windmill,' Millie said.

Larry pored over the locations. For the first time, she could see things clearly.

'That's the boab and I think that's the windmill – near those rocks,' she pointed at the map, 'but the "X" is further east. Hayden, do you remember any junk out that way?'

The pair racked their brains.

'The water on the table boasts a colourful feast, where Hope Springs eternal beneath a hungry rusty beast,' Alice-Miranda recited. 'Could a hungry beast be some kind of digger perhaps? If they made them long enough ago to make sense with this map.'

Larry looked at her brother. 'There's an ancient steam shovel – it was used to build the road to Oodnadatta. Dad said it broke down and was just left there. We haven't been out to that part of the property in ages, but that could be it!'

The children hopped back onto their bikes and Hayden jumped into the ute.

He whistled and Rusty and Blue Dog leapt into the tray. Then he looked at Alice-Miranda. 'Are you coming with me?' he asked.

Millie caught the girl's eye and raised her brows, but Alice-Miranda ignored her. 'Sure,' she said, and scrambled into the cab.

She leaned out of the window as the others mustered beside them. 'And keep a look out for Sprocket.'

The others nodded as Hayden put the ute into gear and led the way.

Chapter 33

Back at Col and Muz's campsite, tempers were flared.

'Surely you can start that blasted ute without the keys,' Wally said. 'Didn't you ever hot-wire anything when you were a kid?'

Muz shook his head.

'You find a way to get that thing started in the next few hours,' he pointed at Col, 'and you can help me with the digging,' he said to Muz. 'What tools have you blokes got?' Wally walked around to the back of the other ute and peered into the tray at the myriad shovels and other bits and pieces. 'These'll do.'

'What are you looking for anyway?' Col asked. 'If it's a mine, then I think that's gonna take a lot longer to find than just a few hours.' He'd been thinking he and Muz had to finish what they'd started and get out of there, before the children and anyone they told about Wally and the bush camp came back. They didn't have time to dig a mine as well.

'It's not a mine, you moron. It's a bag of opals, stolen from a claim years ago and buried out here,' Wally said. He threw a shovel to Muz. 'Follow me.'

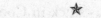

'There!' Alice-Miranda shouted as she spotted something moving behind a mulga tree. But it turned out to be a lone cow.

'Don't worry – if Matilda can be found out here, I'm sure Sprocket can be too,' Hayden called. They continued heading for the steam shovel – although Hayden was worried that he couldn't remember exactly where it was.

He slowed down and shouted at Larry, who was riding along beside them.

The girl rode right up to the window.

'Was there anything else near the steam shovel?' he shouted, hoping for another landmark he could use.

'A bore,' she replied.

Hayden nodded and gave her a thumbs up.

Molly sat beside her husband in the ute and wrapped the handkerchief tightly around her fingers. She had felt sick ever since they'd found Alice-Miranda's note. When she'd called Barnaby and learned that he was stuck in Coober Pedy, and Hugh Kennington-Jones was at the hospital with his brother-in-law who'd been bitten by a snake, it was almost too much to bear. Then the woman had learned someone was out there sabotaging their bores. Now she was in shock.

'We've gotta find the kids,' she mumbled. 'Whoever has Sprocket McGinty might be dangerous and I could never forgive myself if anything happened to them.'

She wished Barnaby were here with the chopper, but apparently he'd seen a warning light shortly after taking off this morning, and had returned to the airport. The mechanic had been working on the helicopter for the past few hours.

Ralph leaned across and patted his wife's leg. 'They'll be okay, love. Hayden and Larry are smart kids.' They'd been following the children's tracks for twenty minutes now. So far, it had been an easy path to follow.

'Yes, but they're just children,' Molly shook her head. 'When I get hold of those blasted kids,' she started.

'What are you gonna do?' Ralph asked.

He saw his wife's face crumple. 'I'm gonna hug the breath right out of all of them.'

A pinched smile came to Ralph's lips. 'You do that, Molly Robinson. You do exactly that.'

Chapter 34

It was fortunate Muz was skinny. Between him and Wally – who hadn't done much more than bark instructions – they'd managed to chip away at the hole between the rocks at the base of the windmill to create an opening large enough for Muz to squeeze through.

'It should be just down there somewhere,' Wally said.

'What is it again?' Muz called out, shining the torch around the crevice.

'I dunno exactly. A small chest, a leather pouch? Something containing precious gems?'

'There's nothing here,' Muz shouted, then turned and realised that wasn't quite right. A snakeskin about eight feet long sat at his feet. He shuddered and scrambled back up through the gap to the surface. He didn't want to run into the owner.

'Geez!' Wally stamped his foot like a petulant toddler. 'It's supposed to be the place.'

'What made you think there was treasure down there?' Muz asked.

Wally explained about the map and recited the rhyme.

Muz looked at him with a toothy grin. 'Well, clearly you've got the wrong spot.'

'And what would you know, genius?' Wally spat, his eyes narrow and mean.

'That rhyme for a start. Windmills aren't hungry, but steam shovels are. They munch things like the ground and rocks and anything in their path,' Muz blathered. 'You should be looking under the old one at the bore we're heading for tomorrow.' The man produced a map with annotated drawings all over it of the bores and other landmarks on Hope Springs.

'Well, stop talking and let's go,' Wally ordered, just as Col fired the engine on the ute. He'd been tinkering for half an hour and, unlike Muz, Col had a misspent youth of joyriding in cars that weren't his own.

Wally leapt into the passenger seat, yelling at Col to go. Muz leapt onto the tray, grabbing the rollbar just before Col planted his foot on the accelerator and turned the ute full circle.

A spiral of dust flew into the air as they sped off across the bumpy plains in search of buried treasure.

'There it is!' Alice-Miranda pointed as the rusty steam shovel appeared in the distance. She could see the chimney stack poking out from the decaying roof, the levers and pulleys of the arm and the huge old bucket resting on the ground.

As the group neared the ancient beast, they were surprised to see another ute. This one was red and a much older model than those they'd seen lately.

'Considering we're in the middle of nowhere, there certainly are a lot of vehicles,' Alice-Miranda said with a frown. 'Any idea who that belongs to?'

Hayden shook his head. He was sure he'd never seen that car before. He parked beside the steam shovel and the others pulled up next to him.

'So this is where we find the lost treasure of Hope Springs?' Alice-Miranda said as they left the car.

'Maybe,' Hayden grinned.

Larry and the others hopped off their bikes.

'What do we do now?' Millie asked. 'I can't imagine there's a magical chasm in the ground that's just going to open up and reveal its sparkling opal reef.'

Something caught Jacinta's eye on the other side of the red ute. She'd wandered away to take a look. 'Hey, I think you're wrong about that!'

The others ran around to where she was standing on top of a mound of dirt, next to a hole with a metal ladder poking out the top.

'Are you kidding me?' Larry said.

Alice-Miranda looked at the shaft and back at the ute. 'There must be someone down there.'

Chapter 35

Taipan Dan rubbed his head and wondered if he was dreaming again. He thought he'd heard voices, but that wasn't possible: he was alone out here, in the middle of nowhere. The irony wasn't lost on him that he was already far more than six feet under.

The pain in his leg was bad but he had to make one last attempt at the ladder. If he could get to the truck and the radio, then maybe he could stop thinking like a dead man. Of course he'd have to explain why he'd been on Hope Springs later, but that was the last of his worries at the moment. He'd just say he was lost – thought it was public property. Bought a claim from an old bloke but the wind must have carried the paperwork away.

Dan managed to push himself up, but fell straight back down again when he heard the voice.

'Hellooo, is anyone there?'

It was a child. A girl.

He tried to speak, but his mouth was drier than the Simpson Desert and the words just wouldn't come.

'Hellooo,' the voice called again.

Dan reached for the water bottle and unscrewed the lid. There was only enough left to moisten his lips. Finally he called back.

'Help,' he muttered weakly.

On the surface, Alice-Miranda held her hand up for the others to be quiet.

'Listen,' she said. 'Did you hear that?'

'Help me.' The voice was barely more than a rasp.

The children looked at one another in surprise. They hadn't been sure what to expect, but a voice calling for help wasn't top of anyone's list.

'We're coming!' Alice-Miranda shouted. 'Sit tight and we'll be down in a minute.'

Larry dropped her backpack to the ground and opened the zip, reaching for a torch.

Lucas had already retrieved his, and a small first-aid kit.

'Come on, let's go,' Larry said, shining the light into the shaft. There was no sign of anyone at the base of the ladder, but the mine likely opened out further in another direction.

The children quickly decided that three would go and three would stay. Alice-Miranda spun and climbed onto the first rung, clenching a small metal torch in her mouth. She'd grabbed her backpack, which contained a water bottle and some food. The light bounced around the red earth as she descended into the cavity, Larry and Lucas following. A shower of grit from Larry's shoes sprinkled onto the top of Alice-Miranda's head. When she reached the bottom, she jumped to the ground and took the torch from her teeth, shining it into the darkness.

'Oh my goodness,' the child gasped as she

caught sight of the elderly man, his back hard up against the mine wall. A trickle of dry blood ran from his forehead down to his bushy grey beard. His cheeks were hollow and there were dark circles under his eyes. His leg was twisted at an alarming angle from the knee.

But it was his hand that caught her off guard. The man's right forefinger was bent over at the top, and the nail looked like a parrot's beak. Alice-Miranda's mind was racing. Surely that wasn't a common trait. Could it be possible that after all these years, this was Chester Lewis?

'You poor man,' she said. 'We need to get you some help right away.'

The man's grey eyes met hers. 'Am I dead?'

Alice-Miranda smiled at him and shook her head. 'No, sir. You're very much alive,' she said, as Larry hopped down beside her and Lucas after that. 'I'm Alice-Miranda Highton-Smith-Kennington-Jones, and this is my cousin Lucas Ridley and our friend Larry Lewis, and we're very pleased to have found you.'

She was sure the man flinched when she mentioned Larry's surname – and not just from the pain in his leg.

'May we know your name, sir?' she asked.

'Dan,' he replied. 'They call me . . .'

'Taipan Dan,' the three children replied in unison, then grinned.

'We know a bossy ginger cat who's going to be very pleased to see you,' Lucas said.

Dan's eyebrows jumped up. 'Junie? You've found Junie?'

Larry nodded. 'She and our dog Rusty are in love, but I guess she'll have to go home once you're well again and you tell us what you were doing trespassing on Hope Springs.'

Tears welled in Dan's eyes. 'That's the best news I've heard for ages.' He paused. 'I guess that's the only news I've heard in ages.'

'Can you move at all?' Alice-Miranda asked.

'I've tried, but my leg's not too good,' he said.

'Don't worry. We'll get help,' she said. 'First we need to find something to make a splint.' After some hushed words with Lucas and Larry, the pair scrambled to the top of the ladder to do exactly that, leaving Alice-Miranda and Dan alone.

She knelt down beside him.

'You're not trespassing, are you?' the child said.

Dan looked at her. 'I shouldn't be here, if that's what you're asking.'

'But you're a Lewis, aren't you?' Alice-Miranda said. The words must have felt like a blow to the man, who slumped backwards. 'You're Chester.'

'How on earth . . .?' the man started, but could barely speak. Alice-Miranda unscrewed the lid of her drink bottle and offered it to him. He took a gulp.

'The others don't know,' Alice-Miranda said. 'I found a diary in Uncle Barnaby's study. It was written by your brother and I've been wondering what to do about it.'

'Evan,' the man rasped. 'He must have hated me for leaving. He never wanted the farm. But I had to go – there was no choice. My wife . . . my son . . .' Tears welled in the old man's eyes. 'I only came back for the opals. I've never cared about the money – it's all gone to the Flying Doctors and the hospital. With this one last pay day they can build a ward for the tiny babies. The only thing I want is it named for Willa and our boy. Their legacy.'

'Oh, Mr Lewis,' Alice-Miranda reached out to hold his hand. 'I don't know how to tell you this – but your boy didn't die along with your wife.

He's alive. His name is Barnaby Lewis and you have two grandchildren – you just met Larry, and there's Hayden as well.'

Dan wondered whether he was dreaming. Surely the head knock was causing him to hallucinate. 'You're wrong,' he said. 'The doctor said my boy died that night same as his mother.'

Alice-Miranda shook her head. 'For some reason he lied to you. I'm so sorry.'

Tears streamed down the man's face as he tried to comprehend the girl's words. 'Oh my goodness, what have I done?' He nursed his forehead in his hands.

'There!' Molly exclaimed.

A scrawny fellow with limbs the colour of snow charged out from a clump of bushes just as they were about to speed past.

'Help!' he yelled. 'Help!'

The fellow ran towards the car, catching Molly off guard. He opened her door and pressed his palms together as if in prayer. 'Hallelujah!' he declared and fell to his knees.

'Are you Sprocket McGinty?' the woman asked.

He jumped up and nodded, then took a bow, waving his hand around as he spoke. 'At your service, madam.'

Ralph leapt out and ran to the passenger side of the car.

'What happened, mate?' he asked.

'Well, how long have you got?' Sprocket began. 'Last weekend I was doing some work on the dugout when . . .'

Ralph rolled his eyes. 'No, what happened out here? Who took you and what did they want?'

Sprocket looked at him. 'Oh. You only want the most recent history.'

There was a crackle through the radio.

'Hope Springs Three to Hope Springs One. Dad, are you listening? Over.' The voice was loud and clear.

Molly grabbed the handset.

'Hayden Lewis, is that you?' she asked, forgetting any call-sign protocols.

'Molly!' the boy gasped. 'Molly, where are you? Over.'

The woman quickly explained that they'd been following the children's tracks and had just found Sprocket McGinty in the middle of nowhere.

Hayden told her they'd located a man who was injured down a mine shaft near the steam shovel. His leg was broken and they couldn't move him.

Molly said she'd call the Flying Doctors, and that she and Ralph were on their way.

'Why haven't you kids been answering your radios?' the woman asked.

'Batteries are almost dead,' Hayden said. 'Got to go. See you soon. Over.'

'Over and out,' Molly replied. Sprocket climbed over the top of the startled woman to straddle the gear stick, perched on the centre console.

'Well, what are we waiting for?' Sprocket said.

Ralph ran back around to the driver's seat and jumped in.

'Do you know how to get there,' Molly asked.

'I certainly do,' Ralph said, as they sped away to the east.

Meanwhile, Wally, Col and Muz had been listening in on the radio. They didn't know if they were ahead of this new car or behind, but hearing the chatter had done nothing to improve Wally's mood.

'Those rotten kids,' he fumed. More people on their way could ruin everything.

'We really don't want any part of your plans,' Muz said. 'You can keep your money.'

'It's too late now. You blokes are in it up to your eyeballs – so whatever I say goes,' Wally said.

'I think the odds are in our favour,' Muz said. 'Two against one.'

'If you say so.' Wally turned to Muz with a sinister grin. 'But just remember, I'm a world champion grudge holder. It might take a week, it may take a year, or, as in this case, it could take more than thirty, but one of these days I'll find you both and you'll regret not doing the right thing by me.'

Muz felt a shiver run down his spine. Col swallowed hard and wished they'd never set foot on Hope Springs – no matter how much they were being paid.

Chapter 36

Molly, Ralph and Sprocket arrived at the steam shovel in a cloud of dust.

It was Sprocket who was out of the vehicle first, this time clambering over the top of Ralph, who was just as shocked as Molly had been when the man had climbed in over her on the way in.

'Sprocket!' Millie called, and raced towards the man. 'It's good to see you.'

'Yes, I know it is,' he said. 'Thought I was a dead man. Still might be if we don't catch that monster who kidnapped me – and knocked me out. At least this time it wasn't with his fist. I thought he was being kind, making me a cuppa. It was just lucky I escaped when he slowed down.'

'You mean Wally,' Millie said.

'You know him?' Sprocket reeled.

'He and his wife run the Kulgera Roadhouse,' the girl replied.

Sprocket frowned. He hadn't been up that way in years, but now that she mentioned the name it did sound vaguely familiar.

Hayden had run to greet Molly and Ralph and, true to her word, the woman just about squeezed the life out of the boy, holding him tightly for several minutes.

'Where's your sister?' the woman asked.

Hayden explained that Larry, Lucas and Alice-Miranda were back at the bottom of the mine with Dan.

'Well, the Flying Doctors aren't going to be here for a while, I'm afraid,' the woman said. 'We have to get him to the homestead if we can.'

Ralph made his way into the shaft and was greeted by Larry with great enthusiasm. She introduced

Alice-Miranda and Lucas before the man's attention turned to Dan.

'Geez, mate, you've done a number on yourself there,' Ralph said, wondering how hard it was going to be to get the injured man up the ladder. But he was a bushman and it wouldn't be the first time he'd had to innovate.

Sprocket McGinty climbed down too. When he reached the bottom he promptly burst into tears.

'Dan, my old matey, you are a sight for sore eyes,' he said, and fell to his knees for the second time that afternoon.

'Mr Sprocket, do you need a tissue?' Alice-Miranda pulled one from her pocket and passed it to him.

He mopped his tears then promptly fired into action.

'Can you hold onto me, Dan?' Sprocket asked. 'I can give you a piggy back up.'

It seemed unlikely, given the poor fellow was so weak. At least his leg was stable, thanks to Alice-Miranda, Larry and Lucas, who had used a length of wood Hayden and the others had found in the back of Wally's ute and the bandages from the first-aid kit to make a splint.

'Are you sure you can hold him?' Alice-Miranda asked.

'Carried a buck kangaroo out of one of my shafts a few months ago. Silly sod fell in. Had to use occy straps but we made it – him kicking up a right old fuss too. How d'ya think I got those scratches on my neck?'

'I thought you said that was from when you were raised by dingoes,' Lucas said.

Ralph chuckled. 'Raised by dingoes, my hairy armpit.'

The children fell about laughing and even Dan managed a grin.

'Well, laugh you may, but help him up and I'll have him out of here in a jiffy. The rest of you make sure that you climb up right behind us so you can cushion the fall if I misstep,' Sprocket said. The children and Ralph looked at each other, wondering if he was serious.

'What are you fellas doing down there?' Molly called. 'We need to get a move on. Someone's coming and I don't think it's help.' It was Jacinta who had spied a vehicle. It was still a way off but it wouldn't take too long to get to them.

The children and Ralph helped Dan up on his good leg. Then they put his arms on Sprocket's shoulders, and tied them around the man's neck with some extra bandages. Despite his size and age, Sprocket stepped onto the ladder and climbed the rungs far more nimbly than anyone had expected.

'Argh!' Dan cried when his leg moved, but Sprocket whispered for him to hold on. That they were almost there. It wasn't quite true, but he wanted to be encouraging.

Ralph stood at the bottom of the ladder, watching every painful move, hoping Sprocket didn't slip and that Dan could hold on.

'Do you think he's found anything down here?' Lucas shone the torch around the walls. There was a line of quartz, but no evidence of any colour.

'He's been here a while if he dug this from scratch,' Larry said. 'It's an impressive hole, even though he has no right to be here.'

Alice-Miranda wondered how Larry and Hayden would react when they found out the truth.

Sprocket took his final step on the top rung of the ladder and hauled Dan out. Hayden, Jacinta and Millie helped lay the man down on the ground while Molly watched the swirl of dust get closer and closer.

'Come on, kids, we need to get moving,' Ralph called from halfway up.

'Get him in the ute,' Molly urged. 'Hurry.'

But by the time Alice-Miranda and the others had reached the surface, Wally had arrived, and he wasn't in the mood to let anyone leave before he had exactly what he'd come for.

Chapter 37

'G'day, kids,' Wally sneered. 'Can't say it's good to see you again, 'cause I don't like tellin' lies.'

In the background, Muz and Col were looking particularly uncomfortable, hopping from one leg to the other and swatting at flies.

Wally turned to them. 'Get *all* the keys.' The two men didn't move. 'Now!'

They scrambled around to the vehicles and did as they were ordered. 'Give 'em to me,' Wally said, then shoved each set into his pockets. 'And lock those two mutts up as well. Put 'em in the dog cage.'

Wally turned and spotted Dan lying on the ground.

'Well, well, well, fancy seeing you here,' he said as a fly buzzed into his mouth. He spat it back out right beside Dan's head.

'Do you two know each other?' Sprocket asked. 'I suppose it would stand to reason seeing as though we ran into each other at Dan's place and you were going through his cupboards and making a general mess. Oh and thanks for the tea this morning.' He rolled his eyes.

'Keep your trap shut, old timer,' Wally said.

Molly and Ralph recognised the man from somewhere, but couldn't place the spot until Alice-Miranda piped up.

'Is this what your wife meant the other day when we met you at the roadhouse? When she said your ship was about to come in? Was she talking about the treasure?' Alice-Miranda looked at the man, whose face seemed to have almost reached boiling point.

'I have a score to settle, sweetheart,' he said. 'You see this bloke here? When he moved to Coober

Pedy he cosied up to my old man. Became the son he wanted and replaced the one he already had. They were as thick as thieves, those two, and when my father kicked the bucket, guess who got his fortune. Him, not me. I got a box of paperwork. Shoved it in the back room and left it there until we sold up. That's when I found something. A diary and papers – all about the treasure at Hope Springs. How he and Dan here were going to find it one day. Dad had one half of the map, so I figured Dan had the other, but he just had that stupid riddle.'

'You sound bitter,' Millie said, garnering herself a glare.

'Just getting what should have been mine from the start,' he said. 'Found anything down there yet, Dan?'

The man shook his head.

'You've gone to an awful lot of effort – must have taken months to dig this pit, and all the while you've been looking in the wrong spot. What a dummy,' Wally sneered. 'It's not a mine you're looking for – it's a bag of stolen gems.'

'I don't understand how you think you're going to get away with any of this,' Alice-Miranda said. 'We all know where you live.'

'You're a clever little thing, aren't you? You seriously think I would have come all this way without an escape plan? Roadhouse is sold – new owner took over a few days ago. By the time anyone finds you lot, Shazza and I will be long gone,' he said.

Col and Muz, ordered by Wally, collected the children's packs and radios, throwing them into the back of the brute's ute. Wally walked to the edge of the mine shaft, grabbing the torch from Larry on the way. The girl kicked him in the shins, but his legs were like concrete and he just laughed it off.

'Why are you doing this?' the girl demanded.

'Do I have to repeat myself for the slow learners?' He sneered at Larry, who was mightily offended by that statement.

'All of you – down that hole,' he motioned at the shaft opening. 'Now!'

Sprocket McGinty was the first to disappear, closely followed by Jacinta. Lucas went after her, then Millie and Larry. Molly and Ralph were next, but Alice-Miranda and Hayden hung back.

'Dan's badly injured. You can't expect him to go back down there,' the girl said. 'He can't walk. His leg's fractured.'

'Boohoo. He can stay here and watch me find what he couldn't then,' Wally said. He shoved Hayden towards the edge. The boy stood up taller and lunged at the man, who knocked him sideways.

'Don't touch my friend!' Alice-Miranda shouted. She ran to Hayden, who was nursing hurt pride rather than anything more serious.

'Stop wasting my time and get down there, you little brats!' he yelled.

Reluctantly, the children did as they were told. The family and friends huddled together at the bottom of the shaft, having managed to squirrel a couple of torches down with them but nothing else.

Molly hugged Jacinta, who was crying. 'I can't believe this is happening,' the girl sobbed.

'Stop it!' Millie ordered. 'All you've done is whine and moan ever since we got here. We're all in this together, if you haven't noticed, and I'm just as scared of the snakes and the lizards as you are – but you don't see me going on about it all the time.'

This was news to Jacinta. She didn't think Millie was afraid of anything.

Alice-Miranda intervened. 'Come on, we have to take care of each other. As soon as they leave we can head back up.'

Except that, as she spoke, the ladder began to rise.

'Pull!' Wally shouted.

'Sorry, kids,' Muz called. Seconds later, their only means of escape was gone.

'Yeah, sure you are,' Hayden yelled back. 'And you can stop stealing our water too. We know it was you – working for those scoundrels at Saxby Downs!'

Meanwhile on the surface, Wally ordered Col and Muz to begin their search.

'Get digging!'

Col and Muz scampered off to find shovels and picks then headed over to the bucket of the steam shovel.

Chapter 38

'Any ideas how we might get out of here?' Larry said despondently.

'Maybe they'll put the ladder back once they've found what they're looking for?' Millie suggested, but there wasn't much agreement on that.

'I knew when we saw that Chlamyd-whatever that no good would come of this trip!' Jacinta sighed.

Molly looked at the girl. 'You saw a frill-necked lizard out here?'

Jacinta nodded. 'Hayden and Larry said you're not a fan.'

'No, siree,' the woman said. 'Greedy so-and-sos, they are.'

'I've got a plan,' Sprocket said, holding a torch beneath his chin to light up his craggy face. 'Let's tell ghost stories.'

'No,' Jacinta said. 'Are you mad?'

'Probably, but I thought it might pass the time,' the man said.

For a little while no one spoke, until the silence became claustrophobic.

'I've got a better idea,' Sprocket said, to groans from everyone else. 'No, hear me out. What was that riddle again?'

The children repeated it for his benefit.

'Let's look for opals,' he said.

Millie shrugged. They had nothing to lose.

'We need to get out so we can help Dan,' Alice-Miranda said, but Sprocket wasn't listening. He'd passed his torch to Ralph and was already chipping away with one of Dan's picks.

Alice-Miranda shone the other torch up the shaft. While Col and Muz had taken the ladder, they hadn't removed the windlass and the bucket.

It was still perched over the top, high above them. If only they could reach it somehow, they might be able to rig up a pulley system.

Jacinta was staring upwards too, doing some mental calculations.

'I can get out!' she declared. The others looked at her.

'How?' Millie said.

'I've got to be good for something on this trip. I'm sorry I've been a terrible whiner. It's just that everything's so different out here. But I'm a gymnast, remember. Last month when I went to that special camp, there was one of those ninja-style courses and something we had to do was shimmy up a round pipe – I was the best at it by a mile. This can't be too different.'

Alice-Miranda smiled at her friend. 'If anyone can do it, you can.'

'How are you going to get up there in the first place?' Molly asked. She wasn't keen on the idea at all, but there didn't seem any alternative and the girl sounded confident.

'She can stand on my shoulders,' Lucas said, but it turned out he wasn't tall enough and neither was Ralph. They needed Sprocket, who was focused on his opal hunt.

Alice-Miranda walked over to the man. 'Mr Sprocket, we need your help,' she said. He ignored her and kept picking away. Alice-Miranda remembered that her father had said once Sprocket was distracted there was no getting his attention until he'd finished what he was doing, so she decided to try another angle.

'He's gone weird again,' Jacinta said, looking upwards and wondering if there was another way.

'Just give me a minute,' Alice-Miranda said. and grabbed the other pick. She hurried over to join him.

Alice-Miranda chipped at the rock face without success. She decided to change tack and moved to the very end of Dan's pit, where it felt as if the walls were damp. She sunk the pick into the rock face with a blow so hard it got stuck.

'Here,' Hayden said, grabbing the end to pull it back out again.

Alice-Miranda held the torch while the boy pushed and pulled and finally dislodged the tool along with a large piece of rock.

'Anything?' Hayden asked as she bent down to pick it up.

'I think it's a pretty piece of potch,' she replied, and tossed it on the ground. It was Millie who saw the flash. She ran to pick it up and turned it over.

'Alice-Miranda. I think you might want to see this,' the girl said, a smile on her lips.

Molly, Ralph and the other kids gathered around while Sprocket hammered away in the darkness.

Ralph shone the light on the rock, which only just fit in the palm of Millie's hand.

'Might be worth a few dollars, but that's nothing to get excited about,' the man said.

The girl turned the rock over and a blaze of emerald green with splashes of blues and reds surprised them all.

'Wow!' the children all gasped.

'So the legend is true, after all,' Molly said. 'We'd heard about this for years – your great-grandfather Charlie said that a surveyor reckoned the place had gemstones like nothing he'd ever seen before, but the pair had a falling out and then the surveyor bloke up and died. The surveyor had put the map in the book he made and added a riddle to punish old Charlie, but it became a bit of a joke – no one thought it was real. About forty years ago, though, half the page went missing.

There was another story that did the rounds too: that there was a robbery in Coober Pedy and the fella who did it hid the bag of gems out here somewhere – but then he turned up dead and no one knew where he'd left them.

'What do you think it could be worth?' Larry asked.

Molly shook her head, unsure.

Alice-Miranda had gone back to the section where she'd found the stone. She shone the torch on the wall and drew in a breath.

'There's more!' she shouted. The family and friends charged over to see and were mesmerised. Below the chunk that Hayden had removed was a wide seam of colour, and who knew how long it ran.

'Mr Sprocket!' the child called. 'We've found something and you're going to want to see it.'

But the man continued chipping at his own spot until Alice-Miranda waved the opal under his nose.

Sprocket stopped and grabbed the stone.

'Oh my word.' He jumped from one leg to the other. 'Dan really was onto something. Woohoo!' The man let out a howl of happiness.

'Shhh!' Alice-Miranda demanded. 'Not so loud. I've got an idea and it's only going to work if everyone sticks exactly to the plan.'

Sprocket nodded and everyone gathered around to listen. Half an hour later, the group had more opals in their pockets than they'd ever seen in their life.

Then, after standing on Sprocket's shoulders, Jacinta managed to shimmy her way up the shaft, her legs almost in a splits position at times. Lucas couldn't watch. The thought that she might fall was too much.

The bucket was hanging inside the shaft, not far from the top. Reaching it, Jacinta tested to see that it was latched in position before she grabbed hold of it and pulled herself up the rope and out onto the ground above.

She lay on her stomach and looked back down into the mine, shocked to see Sprocket McGinty scaling the opening too, his legs spread wide and his hands pushing against the walls. He grabbed the bucket and hauled himself out after her.

'Forgot I was once an elite gymnast myself. Just didn't realise that I should try until I saw you give it a crack,' he grinned, almost blinding the girl.

Jacinta smiled back at the man. He was barking mad for sure, but thank goodness for that.

Over near the steam shovel, the dirt was piling up and tempers were frayed.

'Deeper!' Wally ordered. They could just glimpse him through the cover of the vehicles.

The pair pushed the ladder back to the edge of the hole and Sprocket whispered for everyone to clear the area below. Then he lowered it, holding on as long as he could until the thing flew out of his hands and hit the bottom. Within a minute, the family and friends were out. Sprocket climbed back down alone.

Ralph and the kids pulled the ladder out and hid on the other side of Dan's mullock heap, while Molly went to make sure that Dan was still with them. The man was lying in the back of their ute with the tailgate down. She snuck up on him, finger pressed to her lips and was pleased to see his eyes flicker open. She grabbed a water bottle and moistened his lips. 'Thanks, Molly,' the man croaked. The old woman was staring at him when the realisation hit.

'Oh my word,' she gasped, and turned away, her hand clasped over her mouth. Molly sank to the ground out of sight.

'Hey, Wally!' Sprocket's voice echoed out of the shaft. 'I think we found what you're looking for!' He had to call a few times before the man paid any attention, but then, given they were having no success near the steam shovel, Wally stormed over to the edge.

'What are you talking about, old timer?' Wally snarled.

'Your opals. They're down here,' Sprocket called. 'You're the one looking in the wrong place. It's not a pouch of stolen gems – it's a whole reef.'

The children and Ralph lay against the other side of the mullock heap, hidden from view but ready to leap into action.

'You're delirious, mate. That reef's an old wives tale – the treasure was a bag of stolen gems from Coober Pedy. Saw a newspaper clipping about it in my old man's stuff,' Wally said.

'Suit yourself, but if you send the bucket I'll put one in,' Sprocket said.

'Why would I do that?' Wally spat.

'Because I reckon we've been out here quite a while now and I'm not sure if you know this but the Flying Doctors are on their way,' Sprocket said. 'You don't want to be here then.'

Wally's hands balled into fists and he pulled the pin to lower the bucket.

Sprocket put three small rocks with excellent quality opals into the container and tugged on the rope, signalling to pull it back up.

When Wally saw the light glinting on the find he was mesmerised.

'How much more is there?' the man demanded.

'Enough to make you the richest bloke round these parts and then some,' Sprocket declared. 'Take a look for yourself.'

Wally had no desire to climb down that shaft, but he was desperate to see. He called to Col and Muz.

'If anyone tries to escape, you're gonna cop it, okay,' Wally said as he directed Col and Muz to lower the ladder. The pair were to pull it out again when he reached the bottom.

Seconds later, once Wally had climbed into the mine and the ladder had been retracted, there was a loud fracas down below.

'Where is everyone?' the man demanded. He'd expected to see his prisoners as well as any treasure Sprocket had uncovered.

'I'm a magician,' Sprocket said, shining the torch on the seam, the light causing the rock to sparkle. 'I made them all disappear.'

Wally frowned, completely confused until he caught sight of the seam and was enthralled – which gave Sprocket the opportunity to begin his second climb of the day. His arms and legs were shaking, but he soon reached the top.

'Sprocket!' Wally called, suddenly realising he was alone. 'Where are you, McGinty?' He barrelled up and down the shaft, wondering if there was an exit he'd missed.

The children and Ralph emerged from their hiding spot.

'Well done, Mr Sprocket!' Alice-Miranda ran to give him a hug. There were congratulations all round until Millie realised that Col and Muz had made a getaway.

'Don't worry,' Hayden said. 'They won't be getting far.'

Alice-Miranda grinned and wondered what he'd done. That matter apparently sorted, she charged over to the ute to check on Dan.

'How is he?' she asked Molly, who was kneeling beside him in the back of the tray. Alice-Miranda clambered up next to her.

'He'll be fine. He shouldn't have been here,' Molly balled her fists. 'Not after what he's done.'

Dan reached for the woman's hand, but she pulled it away.

'I think there's more to it, Molly,' Alice-Miranda said. The old woman looked at her quizzically.

'There was nothing to come back for,' Dan whispered.

'What about your son?' the woman said. 'Left to be raised by your brother, a man with a heart of stone.'

'No,' Dan shook his head. 'I swear, the doctor said they'd both died. I was heartbroken. I didn't want to be here,' he said, reaching for Molly again.

This time she didn't turn away – her mind awash with thoughts. If he was telling the truth, the injustice was almost too much to bear.

Alice-Miranda looked at the man and smiled. Sometimes life was so unfair, but now the family could be reunited.

'Come on, you lot, we need to get this silly old fella to the house,' Molly said, turning away from Dan and shaking her head.

'Col, Muz, send that ladder back down!' Wally screamed from inside the mine, but no one was listening to him.

'Do you hear that?' Larry said. In the distance was the whumping sound of helicopter rotors.

Hayden ran to find his backpack and pulled out the flare gun, quickly shooting the rocket into the sky.

Minutes later Barnaby set the chopper down beside the steam shovel and he and Hugh ran to embrace their children.

Chapter 39

Sergeant Ted arrived in a second chopper soon after and the men were hurriedly regaled with the story of Wally and his revenge and everything the children had learned about Col and Muz.

'They won't get far though – not with a cup of water in the diesel tank,' Hayden said with a grin.

Barnaby nodded. 'Well done, mate.'

Larry let Rusty and Blue Dog out of the cage on the back of Wally's ute. The dogs raced around, enjoying their freedom.

Some time later, a convoy of police vehicles arrived to round up the water thieves and take care of Wally. Two constables quickly extracted the man from the mine and handcuffed him, shoving him into the back of the car for the long drive to Coober Pedy.

'You need to secure that shaft,' one of the young police officers said with a smile. 'Wouldn't want anyone else hearing about it.'

'So I believe,' Barnaby said.

'Those other two,' Hugh said. 'They helped you kids?'

'Until Wally got hold of them. They told us they'd had a fight at the Kulgera Roadhouse but when Wally arrived he didn't even mention it. Something was off for sure,' Larry said. 'Alice-Miranda and I saw a toolbox from Saxby Downs in the back of their ute. Millie's got pictures. We think they've been messing with our bores.'

'Great work, kids,' Barnaby said.

'It makes sense why they didn't want anyone to know they'd found Matilda,' Alice-Miranda said. 'They might be foolish and greedy, but I don't think they're mean.'

Barnaby nodded. 'They were probably only doing their boss's bidding.'

'We'll take Dan back with us to Coober Pedy in the chopper,' Sergeant Ted said. 'RFDS is still too far away.'

Barnaby and Hugh walked around to the back of Ralph and Molly's ute, where the old man was lying.

'So you're the legendary Taipan Dan,' Barnaby said. 'Good to meet you. Though I do have a few questions.'

The man blinked, still trying to take everything in. 'You've got your mother's eyes,' he said, a lone tear streaming down his cheek.

Barnaby thought that a strange thing to say, given his mother was Norwegian and he'd always thought her eyes were blue. His own were chocolate brown.

He shook the thought off. 'Come on, we'll get you to hospital,' Barnaby said. Ted and Hugh helped him lift Dan into the second helicopter.

And in that moment Alice-Miranda knew exactly what she had to do. She just had to find the right moment.

By the time the family returned to the homestead it was after dark. Barnaby had taken Molly and Sprocket and gone ahead in the chopper, but the children insisted on riding their bikes and Hugh drove Dan's ute back while Ralph drove his own.

Now they were all seated around the kitchen table filling up on Molly's delicious cottage pie with vegetables, which Sprocket had helped her prepare. Junie was lying on top of Rusty in the corner after having demanded half a bowl of fresh mince, which Sprocket had duly provided. Blue Dog was sitting on the other side of the kitchen – you could almost see her shaking her head. Cam was going to pick her up tomorrow.

'So what's going to happen with the mine, Dad?' Larry asked her father.

Barnaby hadn't given it much thought. 'We're farmers, honey, not miners. But maybe when Dan is well again I'll see if he wants to keep at it – though I'll be interested to know how he knew about it in the first place.'

'He must have had half of that map, and the riddle too,' Hayden said. 'Did he work here when he was young?'

'Maybe he stole it,' Jacinta said.

Alice-Miranda looked across at Molly, who lowered her gaze.

Sprocket grinned. 'I'll help him. We could split the profits. Fifty-fifty.'

Everyone frowned at the man.

'Okay, sixty-forty then.' He revised his figure to great guffaws of laughter.

'Do you need a lift home tomorrow, Sprocket?' Molly asked.

Ralph looked at her. 'We weren't planning on a trip to town, were we?'

'We have to replace all that food Wally stole and I thought I'd look in on Dan at the hospital.'

Alice-Miranda noticed Molly's eyes welling up again. The woman turned away and brushed at the tears.

'I think we'll be fixing bores for another couple of days,' Barnaby said, 'but we might start the mustering – or at least you kids can, if you're up to it.'

There was a rousing chorus of yeses, and even Jacinta agreed. Ralph had heard from Buddy that the pilot would be home tomorrow, which made Barnaby extremely happy. No more flying for him – though he'd surprised himself these past few days.

When dinner was finished, the family and friends spread out across the house to have showers, watch television or head to bed.

Alice-Miranda was walking back from the bathroom in her pyjamas when she saw the light on in Barnaby's study.

She turned down the hall and stood in the doorway.

'Oh, hello sweetheart,' the man said, glancing up from behind the desk. 'Just catching up on some paperwork. Been a big week.'

The girl nodded. 'Uncle Barnaby, you know when I was looking for the other half of that map . . .'

'I still can't believe you actually found it.' He shook his head. 'One of these days I'll have to give the place a proper clean out – never know what you might come across.'

'Actually, I found something else too, and I think you should see it,' the child said, and moved the library ladder around so she could scale to the top and pull out the small dusty tome. 'Perhaps you've read it before?'

'I don't think so,' Barnaby said. He'd once been caught playing on the ladder by his father, and had received such a telling off that he hadn't entered the room again until the old man died.

'I didn't mean to pry. It's just that it had me hooked and it wasn't until the end that I realised the full implications, and it's certainly not fair for me to know and you not to,' the girl said.

Molly walked down the hallway and poked her head inside the door. 'Finished the cleaning up, Barnaby. I'll be off home,' she said, then spotted the book in Alice-Miranda's hand.

'What's that?' she asked.

Alice-Miranda passed it to Barnaby. 'Maybe you should stay and read it too, Molly,' the child said. 'Though I don't think it will be as much of a surprise to you.'

Molly's lips trembled and tears pricked her eyes.

'What are you talking about, Alice-Miranda?' Barnaby said.

'All families have their secrets. But sometimes I think they turn out to be really good ones,' the girl replied. She rushed forward and gave the man a hug, then hugged Molly on the way out.

'What's she talking about, Molly?' Barnaby asked. 'What do you know?'

The woman took Barnaby's hand. 'It's about time,' she said.

He took a deep breath and opened the book, Molly by his side.

A short while later, Barnaby reached his revelation and turned to the woman who had been his second mother. 'You knew?'

'Some of it,' she said. 'I always thought Evan would tell you, but then when he didn't I wasn't sure what to do, so I said nothing. I'm so sorry.'

Barnaby turned, hugging Molly tightly. She hugged him right back – same as she'd always done. Strangely, he wasn't sad. There was something comforting in the knowledge that his mother hadn't abandoned him and his father wasn't the man he'd thought he was. They kept reading to the end, and by the last page Barnaby knew for sure. Life would never be the same again, but there was a very good chance it would be even better.

And just in case you're wondering . . .

Barnaby would never know why the doctor had lied to his father that night. The government laws of the day said the baby would be sent to a children's home, but Molly had tracked the newborn Barnaby down and brought him home to Hope Springs. She was angry that Chester had abandoned his son and was prepared to raise the boy as her own until Charles Lewis, the child's grandfather, took one look at the lad and demanded that his younger son, Evan, return with his new wife to bring up the boy.

Devastated by the loss of his wife and baby, Chester had trudged the length and breadth of the outback for ten years before he found himself in Coober Pedy. He was taken in by Hector, Wally's father, who had fallen out with his own son. Chester told the bloke his name was Dan, and acquired his nickname after his fabled run-in with a taipan. The older man taught 'Dan' everything he knew about mining, but what he couldn't understand was why Dan never had any money.

That was easy. Dan kept enough to pay for his food and provisions, but everything else he earned went anonymously to the Royal Flying Doctor Service and the Coober Pedy hospital. It was the only way he could make sense of losing his wife and son.

He had gone back to Hope Springs for the first time after having come across the old map and riddle when he was cleaning up his dugout one day. If there was as much treasure in that hole as the legend had him believe, he'd be able to donate enough money to the hospital for a whole new neonatal wing – which he would have named in Willa's honour. It would have been her legacy.

Someone had started digging that shaft years ago – likely the surveyor – but it had been long forgotten and, at times, flooded. Perhaps Col and Muz's tampering with the bores had helped to dry it out, the way they were messing with the water table.

Those two blokes were caught about twenty kilometres from the steam shovel with the hood up and cursing their luck. But, in return for giving evidence against their bosses – the new owners of Saxby Downs, who were stealing the water to increase their cattle stocks – the pair was given immunity, and months later Barnaby offered them jobs. After all, no one knew the bores as well as they did and they could do the maintenance twice as fast as anyone else.

Lawrence made a full recovery from his run-in with the western brown snake and returned to the station before the end of the week. Once there, he spent more time helping Molly around the house than out in the field. His agent insisted that it was important for him to stay alive, and Charlotte was very happy with that decision.

The children finished their week of mustering and decided it was one of the best adventures of their lives. Even Jacinta, who had to agree that finding the treasure was incredibly exciting – especially when Barnaby insisted they each keep an opal for themselves. Hayden and Larry hoped they'd get to visit Alice-Miranda and the others at home one of these years, but in the meantime, Alice-Miranda and Hayden planned to write to each other from boarding school. Millie had so many photographs she wasn't sure which one to enter in the competition, but there was a particularly spectacular shot of two eagles flying into a pink sunset. Jacinta said she'd win purely because she'd captured the pterodactyls.

Evie was home much earlier than she'd antici-pated and even got to meet her idol, Lawrence Ridley, the day before he left.

Several months later, once the old man had made a full recovery from his broken leg and sore head, Barnaby brought Dan to live at Hope Springs where he was reunited with Junie and the rest of his family. Hayden and Larry could hardly believe their luck at their grandfather being the legendary Taipan Dan. And better still, he could take them fossicking for opals.

Sprocket McGinty returned home to his dugout, where he completed the renovations and made a start on a whole new guest wing. After all, Hugh with Two promised to come back again soon and bring that kid with four and more.

Glossary

blower a machine like a giant vacuum cleaner, used to suck opal dirt from underground into a pipe, up the shaft and into a waiting truck.

bore a method of bringing groundwater to the surface.

bore water groundwater that has been accessed by drilling a bore into underground water stores.

dugout a home formed by excavating into a rocky hillside.

Great Artesian Basin   the largest and deepest artesian basin in the world, stretching over 1,700,000 square kilometres. The basin provides the only source of fresh water through much of inland Australia.

mullock heap   the piles of valueless dirt pulled out of mining shafts.

muster   the process of gathering livestock together.

opal   a precious, multicoloured gemstone found in many varieties.

pick   a sharp tool used to dig out opal.

potch   a form of non-precious opal that doesn't contain gem colour.

reef   a mythically high concentration of opal. Also called a vein.

seam   a thin horizontal layer of opal. Opal is often found by miners by following a seam.

willy willy   spiralling wind that collects dust.

windlass   a winch used to haul opal dirt up out of a mine.

Cast of characters

The Highton-Smith-Kennington-Jones party

Alice-Miranda Highton-Smith-Kennington-Jones	Only child, ten and a half years of age
Hugh Kennington-Jones	Alice-Miranda's doting father
Millicent Jane McLaughlin-McTavish-McNaughton-McGill	Alice-Miranda's best friend and room mate
Jacinta Headlington-Bear	Friend
Lucas Nixon	Alice-Miranda's cousin
Lawrence Ridley	Lucas's father and Alice-Miranda's uncle

The Lewis household

Barnaby Lewis	Co-owner of Hope Springs Station and friend of Hugh's
Evie Lewis	Co-owner of Hope Springs Station and Barnaby's wife
Hayden Lewis	Son of Barnaby and Evie
Illaria (Larry) Lewis	Daughter of Barnaby and Evie

Rusty	Lewis family dog
Molly Robinson	Beloved worker on Hope Springs station and Ralph's wife
Ralph Robinson	Beloved worker on Hope Springs station and Molly's husband

Others

Wally	Co-owner of the Kulgera Roadhouse and Sharon's husband
Sharon	Co-owner of the Kulgera Roadhouse and Wally's wife
Sprocket McGinty	Eccentric miner from Coober Pedy
Taipan Dan	Miner and local legend
Junie	Taipan Dan's cat
Cameron Darley	Owner of Darley Springs Station and neighbour of the Lewises
Laura Darley	Cameron's wife
Matilda Darley	Four-year-old daughter of Cameron and Laura
Ted Johnson	Police sergeant at Coober Pedy and Laura's brother
Col	Young farm worker
Muz	Young farm worker

About the author

Jacqueline Harvey taught for many years in girls' boarding schools. She is the author of the bestselling Alice-Miranda, Clementine Rose and Kensy and Max series, and was awarded Honour Book in the 2006 Australian CBC Awards for her picture book *The Sound of the Sea*. She now writes full-time and is working on more Alice-Miranda and Kensy and Max adventures, and some exciting new projects too.

jacquelineharvey.com.au

Jacqueline Supports

Jacqueline Harvey is a passionate educator who enjoys sharing her love of reading and writing with children and adults alike. She is an ambassador for Dymocks Children's Charities and Room to Read. Find out more at dcc.gofundraise.com.au and roomtoread.org.

Enter a world of
mystery and adventure in

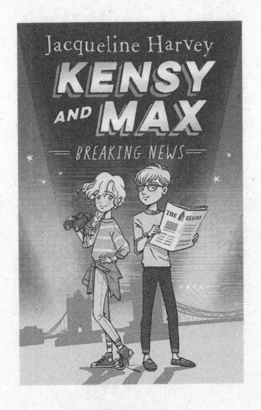

OUT NOW